THE RESURRECTION OF JESUS CHRIST AS THE LAST ADAM

REV. MICHAEL RAY COX SR.

APPRECIATIONS AND ACKNOWLEDGMENTS

As the father of five children, I have a deep appreciation for family life. My beautiful Filipina wife, Evangeline Ofril Escala Cox, is the love of my life. She is also an inspiration and my motivation. She not only encouraged me to finish this book, but also typed all of my written notes for it. I thank her very much for being such an important part of this book. I love you, Honey, until death do us part. Thank you for being a dedicated Christian and motivator for our marriage. In the Name of JESUS CHRIST, our LORD and Savior, to GOD we give all of the praise and the glory and honor and to the HOLY SPIRIT, the Teacher and Guide of GOD's Word. Amen.

I was born and lived in a small town in Springfield (Livingston Parish), Louisiana. My actual place of birth was Independence, Louisiana, in Lallie Kemp Charity Hospital. I was baptized at an early age and attended the Sweet Home Missionary Baptist Church, pastored by the late Rev. Mitchell Williams. I graduated from Springfield High School in 1976.

My parents are Eddie Edward Cox and Gloria Jean Hart Cox. My father was born in Napoleonville, Louisiana, and my mother in New Orleans, Louisiana. I am the fourth of eight children; from the oldest to the youngest: Larry Hart, James Edward Cox, Brenda Ann Cox Betts, Irma Jean Cox Vereen, Karen Ann Cox, Paula Denise Cox, and the late Ronald Ray Cox.

We were reared as a Christian family. I feel so blessed to have a family that loves one another. I thank GOD for all of my friends, brothers-in-law, and sisters-in-law, and I thank GOD for all nine of my grandchildren: Kylah Sharve'y Baker, Kiera Shaney Baker, Harvey Jerard Baker Jr., Jaylen Darnell Thomas, Katelyn Michelle Thomas, Ju'Byes Devon Parker Jr., JaCori Devon Parker, Tobias Mondrell Cox, Jr., Amiyah Cox, and Lylah Cox.

To my loved ones and friends, my parents and grandparents, and to those who had a direct impact in my life, the late Deacon Eddie Edward Cox and

Gloria Jean Hart Cox, I thank you. My father, Eddie Edward Cox, is a great example of a layman who strives to serve GOD with all his heart, soul, and mind, and my mother, Gloria Jean Hart Cox, inspired me to be independent and to love GOD and all people. I also thank my grandfather, the late Deacon James Davis Hart, and my grandmothers, the late Ester Green Hart and the late Emma Harry Roberts.

I want to thank my Heavenly Father for giving me the health, strength, and everything necessary to complete this book.

He blessed me with some wonderful men and women of GOD.

Men like the late Pastor Mitchell Williams, Pastor Leon Merlan, Pastor Elmore Garner, Rev. Charles Doneley, the late Pastor Charles F. Bennett, Deacon James Forrest, Deacon Russell Merical, Deacon David Gaskins, Deacon Jay Hughes, the late bass/guitar player Ricky Hill, the late Deacon Ira Marshall, Pastor Willie Rolland, Rev. Kenneth Owens, Rev. Robertson, Pastor Glenn R. Shields and Pastor James Blake,

Pastor Charles E. Hart, the late Deacon Alton Hart, the late Deacon Benjamin Hart, the late Deacon Roy Cox, the late Deacon Selven Cox, Sr., the late Deacon Wilbert Cox, Pastor Samuel Smith Jr. Ph.D., Deacon Ervin Beavers, Dr. Bernard J. Sutton, a great teacher and Pastor, Rev. Shawn Hawkins, the late Nathaniel Hart Sr., the late Pastor Alfred Lee Hart, Rev. Lawrence Hart, Rev. Samuel Hart, Leon Hart, Dennis Hart, Joseph Hart, Linell Roberts, the late Birvon Roberts Sr., Pastor Kimmon, the late Pastor Ivy Williams, Pastor Bob Hailey, the late Horace Davis, Pastor Wellie White, Pastor Robert Smith, the late Pastor Herbert Garner, the late John Banks, the late Audrey Banks, the late Archie McGee, the late Ezekiel Lockman, Rev. Michael Adams, Rev. Travis Hunt, Rev. Larry Menton, Anthony Vereen Sr, the late Clarence Betts Sr., Samuel Brumfield, James Geathers, my brothers Larry Hart, James Edward Cox, and the late Ronald Ray Cox.

Women such as Brenda Ann Cox Betts—my oldest sister, Irma Jean Cox Vereen—second oldest sister, Karen Cox—third oldest sister, Paula Denise Cox—my baby sister, along with Donna Callahan, Phyllis Ellaine

Lockman Cox, Evangeline Ofril Escala Cox, Jonetta Caldwell, Lula Hart, Betty Hart, Jessie Hart, Blanche Hart, Cynthia Hart, Vicki Hart, Dasha Hart, Warnella Hart Coston, Edna Hart, Gayle Hart, Brenda Roberts, Earline Cox, the late Edna Cox, the late Leola Cox Parker, Sister Ida Louise Williams, Sister Evelina Flecher, Sister L. Perkins, Anna Mae Cox, Ana Johnson, Ritchel Wells, Sarah Wilson, Geraldine Mcgee, the late Gladys Callahan, and Florida Lockman.

Last but not least, I am blessed with my children: Shannon Callahan Baker, Kenisha Callahan Parker, Michael Ray Cox Jr., Airess Padda, Tobias Mondrell Cox, Angel, and all my grandchildren, all my beautiful nieces and nephews, close relatives, and special friends.

Others deserving mention include:

My brother-in-law John Walter Escala, for the cover graphic design.

My wife, Evangeline Escala Cox, for all her help in completing this project.

CONTENTS

i|The Resurrection of Jesus Christ as the Last Adam

INTRODUCTION

My mother was born on August 6, 1937, and she transitioned to heaven on August 11, 1995 where she met her "Ministering Angels", according to **Hebrews 1:13-14**: *"¹³But to which of the angels said he at any time, sit on my right hand, until I make thine enemies thy footstool? ¹⁴Are they not all ministering spirits, sent forth to minister for them who shall be heirs of salvation?"* The Angels took my mother to paradise as they carried Lazarus.

Luke 16:22 tells us, *"²²And it came to pass, that the beggar died, and was carried by the angels into Abraham's bosom: the rich man also died, and was buried"*.

What a delight it will be to meet our guardian angels who have watched over us in our Earthly life. Who will carry us to our Heavenly home? Amen thank you Jesus, my God and Savior. All of my young life I feared death, but when I became a man and studied the Bible, my fear went away because of what Jesus did on the cross. Now, for me, to live is Christ, and to die is to gain.

Philippians 1:12, *"12 But I would ye should understand, brethren, that the things which happened unto me have fallen out rather unto the furtherance of the gospel".*

I was called into the Ministry on March 8, 1998. I was baptized at an early age and I am saved by the grace of God, and I have been studying the word of God ever since. **Hebrews 11:6** states, *"6 But without faith it is impossible to please him: for he that cometh to God must believe that he is, and that he is a rewarder of them that diligently seek him."* One of the subjects in the Bible that I diligently studied was Life after Death. Because I feared death at a young age and had not heard the word preach about death and the process of death, I wanted to know what happened when you die. What happens to your body, what happens to your soul? And what happens to your spirit? According to **1 Thessalonians 5:23,** *"23 And the very God of peace sanctify you wholly; and I pray God your whole spirit and soul and body be preserved* *blameless unto the coming of our Lord Jesus Christ.*" So, in studying the Bible through the Holy Spirit, I learned the process of death. I thank my Lord Jesus, my God and savior, for the new life. I have been studying death ever since my mother, Gloria Jean Hart Cox, transitioned to Heaven exactly 24 years and 7 ago months today, as I pen this book. Rest in paradise until your fourth son, Michael Ray Cox, Sr., meets you again in paradise. I love you and miss you so dearly. It seems like only yesterday. And all of your children miss you dearly, too. Larry, James, Brenda, Michael, Irma, Karen, Paula, and Ronald. Our father, Eddie Cox, transitioned to paradise on April 25,2009. Tribute to our mother.

Mother and Daddy, your time has come to depart from earth. We are saddened, but we know we will see you in the morning, knowing all of this doesn't make it easier to let you go. We all know you are in a better place, and that you are not suffering or in any pain. But it is so hard because you were our mother and father.You taught us how to work hard to get what we want out of life, to be independent and to always stay close, loving and caring. Most of all, you taught us about God, and we know He will carry us through this time. We are totally trusting and believing in just that. Thank you, Mother and Daddy, for all that you did for us. We love you both dearly.

Thank you, my Lord and savior Jesus Christ and my God, for giving me the Holy Spirit and the wisdom that is from above, the knowledge and understanding and the spiritual understanding to write this book. The reason I am writing this book is because the Lord put on my heart to try, with the help of the Holy Spirit, to answer this question about life after death and the process of death. I get asked all the time what happens after death; many Christians ask that question. I had three categories of readers in mind as I sat down to pen this book:

Those who have been asking the question about death; Bible-believing Christians.

Those observers from outside the church, who believe not in Jesus Christ and his resurrection to life.

Most importantly, the preacher that preaches the word of God and the resurrection of Jesus as the last Adam.

For the resurrection of Jesus is the foundational fact on which Christianity is built: *"If Christ be not raised your faith is vain; Ye are yet in your sins"* (**1 Corinthians 15:17**).

The proof of Jesus' "deity" depended on his resurrection from the dead. Five different times Jesus declared that he would be crucified and buried, and on the third day he would rise from dead:

Matthew 12:39-40, *"[39] But he answered and said unto them, an evil and adulterous generation seeketh after a sign; and there shall no sign be given to it, but the sign of the prophet Jonas:*

⁴⁰For as Jonas was three days and three nights in the whale's belly; so, shall the Son of man be three days and three nights in the heart of the earth."

Matthew 20:17-19, *"¹⁷And Jesus going up to Jerusalem took the twelve disciples apart in the way, and said unto them,*

¹⁸Behold, we go up to Jerusalem; and the Son of man shall be betrayed unto the chief priests and unto the scribes, and they shall condemn him to death,

¹⁹And shall deliver him to the Gentiles to mock, and to scourge, and to crucify him: and the third day he shall rise again."

Matthew 26:30-32, *"³⁰And when they had sung a hymn, they went out into the mount of Olives.*

³¹Then saith Jesus unto them, all ye shall be offended because of me this night: for it is written, I will smite the shepherd, and the sheep of the flock shall be scattered abroad.

³²But after I am risen again, I will go before you into Galilee."

Luke 18:31-33, *"³¹Then he took unto him the twelve, and said unto them, Behold, we go up to Jerusalem, and all things that are written by the prophets concerning the Son of man shall be accomplished.*

³²For he shall be delivered unto the Gentiles, and shall be mocked, and spitefully entreated, and spitted on:

³³And they shall scourge him, and put him to death: and the third day he shall rise again."

John 2:19-22, *"¹⁹Jesus answered and said unto them, destroy this temple, and in three days I will raise it up.*

²⁰Then said the Jews, Forty and six years was this temple in building, and wilt thou rear it up in three days?

²¹But he spake of the temple of his body.

²²When therefore he was risen from the dead, his disciples remembered that he had said this unto them; and they believed the scripture, and the word which Jesus had said."

If Jesus had not been raised, we would not have known whether He was what he claimed to be or not, but the Bible declared (demonstrated) him to be the son of God by his resurrection from the dead.

Romans 1:4, *"⁴And declared to be the Son of God with power, according to the spirit of holiness, by the resurrection from the dead".*

My prayers are that Pastors and Preachers and Bishops and Teachers of God's word will teach more clearly about death, explaining the process of what happens after death when we die. I hope that reading this book, *The Resurrection of Jesus as the last Adam,* will help you to do so in the name of Jesus Christ our Lord and my God and our savior, Amen. I would like to once again thank my Lord and savior Jesus Christ for giving me his Holy spirit, the wisdom that is from above, and the knowledge and understanding—the spiritual understanding—to write this book. In Jesus' name, Amen.

ADAM AND EVE IN THE GARDEN

The Scriptures speak of two men. **The first is called ADAM. The second is called the last ADAM or the second man.**

1 Corinthians 15:47, *"The first man is of the earth, earthy; the second man is the Lord from heaven."*

The first Adam is charged with bringing sin into the world.

Romans 5:12, *"Wherefore, as by one man sin entered into the world, and death by sin; and so, death passed upon all men, for that all have sinned".*

The last Adam came to reverse what the first Adam did, and to put away sin.

Hebrews 9:26, *"For then must he often have suffered since the foundation of the world: but now once* *in the end of the world hath he appeared to put away sin by the sacrifice of himself."*

For if by one man's offence death reigned

Romans 5:17, *"For if by one man's offence death reigned by one; much more they which receive abundance of grace and of the gift of righteousness shall reign in life by one, Jesus Christ."*

The First Adam God Created

Genesis 1:26-27 tells us, *"26 And God said, let us make man in our image, after our likeness: and let them have dominion over the fish of the sea, and over the fowl of the air, and over the cattle, and over all the earth, and over every creeping thing that creepeth upon the earth.*

27 So God created man, in his own image, in the image of God created he him; male and female created he them."

From this we see that man is a Created being, that He was made in the image of God. The whole human race is of **"one species"** and had a common origin.

Acts 17:26 says, "*26 And hath made of one blood all nations of men for to dwell on all the face of the earth, and hath determined the times before appointed, and the bounds of their habitation".*

And God formed (fashioned) man of the dust of the ground and breathed into his nostrils "**the breath of life**" and man became a living soul. From this, we see that the creation of man was threefold:

1. **The Body**

2. **The Spirit**

3. **The Soulish part of man.**

The two principal parts of man are the body and the spirit. But the functions of these are separate, one being physical and the other Spiritual. The third part is the soul.

The soul is intermediate between them, through which they may communicate. This makes man a "threefold being" (1 Thessalonians 5:23, Hebrews 4:12).

1 Thessalonians 5:23, *"And the very God of peace sanctify you wholly; and I pray God your **whole spirit and soul and body** be preserved blameless unto the coming of our Lord Jesus Christ."*

Hebrews 4:12, *"For the word of God is quick, and powerful, and sharper than any two-edged sword, piercing even to the **dividing asunder of soul and spirit**, and of the joints and marrow, and is a discerner of the thoughts and intents of the heart."*

In **Adam** as originally created, the "Soul" was such a perfect medium of communication between the "body and the spirit" that there was no conflict between them.

When man fell, **Adam's** soul became the "battlefield of the body and the spirit".

In **Romans 7:7-24,** Paul describes the battler:

"7 What shall we say then? Is the law sin? God forbids. Nay, I had not known sin, but by the law: for I had not known lust, except the law had said, thou shalt not covet.

8 But sin, taking occasion by the commandment, wrought in me all manner of concupiscence. For without the law sin was dead.

9 For I was alive without the law once: but when the commandment came, sin revived, and I died.

10 And the commandment, which was ordained to life, I found to be unto death.

11 For sin, taking occasion by the commandment, deceived me, and by it slew me.

12 Wherefore the law is holy, and the commandment holy, and just, and good.

13 Was then that which is good made death unto me? God forbids. But sin, that it might appear sin, working death in me by that which is good; that sin by the commandment might become exceeding sinful.

¹⁴ For we know that the law is spiritual: but I am carnal, sold under sin.

¹⁵ For that which I do I allow not: for what I would, that do I not; but what I hate, that do I.

¹⁶ If then I do that which I would not, I consent unto the law that it is good.

¹⁷ Now then it is no more I that do it, but sin that dwelleth in me.

¹⁸ For I know that in me (that is, in my flesh,) dwelleth no good thing: for to will is present with me; but how to perform that which is good I find not.

¹⁹ For the good that I would I do not: but the evil which I would not, that I do.

²⁰ Now if I do that I would not, it is no more I that do it, but sin that dwelleth in me.

²¹ *I find then a law, that, when I would do good, evil is present with me.*

²² *For I delight in the law of God after the inward man:*

²³ *But I see another law in my members, warring against the law of my mind, and bringing me into captivity to the law of sin which is in my members.*

²⁴ *O wretched man that I am! who shall deliver me from the body of this death?"*

Eve was not fashioned in the same way as **Adam**. She was made later.

Genesis 2:21-23 states, "*²¹ And the LORD God caused a deep sleep to fall upon Adam, and he slept: and he took one of his ribs, and closed up the flesh instead thereof;*

²² And the rib, which the LORD God had taken from man, made he a woman, and brought her unto the man.

*23 And Adam said, this is now **bone of my bones, and flesh of my flesh**: she shall be called Woman, because she was taken out of Man".*

The reason why **Eve** was not fashioned separately from **Adam**, but was taken out of Adam's side, was to show that in their relation to each other as man and wife they were to be **one flesh**. They were to be one, and physically they were to be counterparts of each other.

Adam and Eve are a type of the **last Adam** and his wife—the Church.

Ephesians 5:25-32:

"25 Husbands, love your wives, even as Christ also loved the church, and gave himself for it;

26 That he might sanctify and cleanse it with the washing of water by the word,

27 That he might present it to himself a glorious church, not having spot, or wrinkle, or any such thing; but that it should be holy and without blemish.

²⁸ So ought men to love their wives as their own bodies. He that loveth his wife loveth himself.

²⁹ For no man ever yet hated his own flesh; but nourisheth and cherisheth it, even as the Lord the church:

³⁰ For we are members of his body, of his **flesh, and of his bones.**

³¹ For this cause shall a man leave his father and mother, and shall be joined unto his wife, and they two shall be one flesh.

³² This is a great mystery: but I speak concerning Christ and the church."

Adam was created as a full-grown man, perfect in intellect and knowledge, because he names all the Beasts of the field and the fowls of the air.

Genesis 2:20 states, *"²⁰ And Adam gave names to all cattle, and to the fowl of the air, and to every beast of the field; but for Adam there was not found a help meet for him."*

In the Garden: **Genesis 2:8-15** tells us,

"*8 And the L*ORD* God planted a garden eastward in Eden; and there he put the man whom he had formed.*

*9 And out of the ground made the L*ORD* God to grow every tree that is pleasant to the sight, and good for food; the tree of life also in the midst of the garden, and the tree of knowledge of good and evil.*

10 And a river went out of Eden to water the garden; and from thence it was parted, and became into four heads.

*11 The name of the first is **Pison**: that is, it which compasseth the whole land of Havilah, where there is gold;*

12 And the gold of that land is good: there is bdellium and the onyx stone.

*13 And the name of the second river is **Gihon**: the same is it that compasseth the whole land of Ethiopia.*

¹⁴ *And the name of the third river is **Hiddekel***: *that is, it which goeth toward the east of Assyria. And the fourth river is **Euphrates.***

¹⁵ *And the L*ORD *God took the man, and put him into the garden of Eden to dress it and to keep it."*

Adam and Eve were equal in the Garden. God has no respect of person, as **James 2:1** tells us: "My brethren, have not the faith of our Lord Jesus Christ, the Lord of glory, with respect of persons.

Leviticus 19:15 says, "¹⁵ Ye shall do no unrighteousness in judgment: thou shalt not respect the person of the poor, nor honor the person of the mighty: but in righteousness shalt thou judge thy neighbour."

But because of sin, the woman's sentence was that she should lose her position as man's equal and become subject to him, to Adam.

In Genesis 3:16, "¹⁶ *Unto the woman he said, I will greatly multiply thy sorrow and thy conception; in* *sorrow thou shalt bring forth children; and thy desire shall be to thy husband, and he shall rule over thee."*

1 Corinthians 11:3, *"³ But I would have you know, that the head of every man is Christ; and the head of the woman is the man; and the head of Christ is God."*

Ephesians 5:22, *"²² Wives, submit yourselves unto your own husbands, as unto the Lord."*

1 Timothy 2:12-15, *"¹² But I suffer not a woman to teach, nor to usurp authority over the man, but to be in silence.*

¹³ For Adam was first formed, then Eve.

¹⁴ And Adam was not deceived, but the woman being deceived was in the transgression.

¹⁵ Notwithstanding she shall be saved in childbearing, if they continue in faith and charity and holiness with sobriety."

But because of sin, Adam's sentence was given in Genesis 3:17: *"¹⁷ And unto Adam he said, because thou hast hearkened unto the voice of thy wife, and hast eaten of the tree, of which I commanded thee, saying, Thou shalt not eat of it: cursed is the ground for thy sake; in sorrow shalt thou eat of it all the days of thy life"*.

Genesis 1:26 *"²⁶ And God said, let us make man in our image, after our likeness: and* **let them have dominion** *over the fish of the sea, and over the fowl of the air, and over the cattle, and over all the earth, and over every creeping thing that creepeth upon the earth."*

Genesis 9:2, *"[2] And the fear of you and the dread of you shall be upon every beast of the earth, and upon every fowl of the air, upon all that moveth upon the earth, and upon all the fishes of the sea; into your hand are they delivered."*

Genesis 9:6, *"[6] Whoso sheddeth man's blood, by man shall his blood be shed: for in the image of God made the man."*

Psalm 8:6-9, "*⁶ Thou madest him to have domin-ion over the works of thy hands; thou hast put all things under his feet:*

⁷ All sheep and oxen, yea, and the beasts of the field;

⁸ The fowl of the air, and the fish of the sea, and whatsoever passeth through the paths of the seas.

⁹ O Lord our Lord, how excellent is thy name in all the earth!"

Adam lost his dominion to the god of this world, which is the Devil.

2 Corinthians 4:4, "*⁴In whom the god of this world hath blinded the minds of them which believe not, lest the light of the glorious gospel of Christ, who is the image of God, should shine unto them."*

Luke 4:1-13 describes how when Adam sins, he delivers the world over to Satan. Reference verse Luke 4:5-6:

"**1** And Jesus being full of the Holy Ghost returned from Jordan, and was led by the Spirit into the wilderness,

2 Being forty days tempted of the devil. And in those days, he did eat nothing: and when they were ended, he afterward hungered.

3 And the devil said unto him, if thou be the Son of God, command this stone that it be made bread.

4 And Jesus answered him, saying, it is written, that man shall not live by bread alone, but by every word of God.

5 And the devil, taking him up into a high mountain, shewed unto him **all the kingdoms of the world** in a moment of time.

6 And the devil said unto him, all this power will I give thee, and the glory of them: for that is delivered unto me; and to whomsoever I will I give it.

7 If thou therefore wilt worship me, all shall be thine.

8 *And Jesus answered and said unto him, get thee behind me, **Satan**: for it is written, thou shalt worship the Lord thy God, and him only shalt thou serve.*

9 *And he brought him to Jerusalem, and set him on a pinnacle of the temple, and said unto him, if thou be the Son of God, cast thyself down from hence:*

10 *For it is written, He shall give his angels charge over thee, to keep thee:*

11 *And in their hands, they shall bear thee up, lest at any time thou dash thy foot against a stone.*

12 *And Jesus answering said unto him, it is said, thou shalt not tempt the Lord thy God.*

13 *And when the devil had ended all the temptation, he departed from him for a season."*

Hebrews 2:8, *"**8** Thou hast put all things in subjection under his feet. For in that he put all in* *subjection under him, he left nothing that is not put under him. But now we see not yet all things put under him."*

James 3:7, *"7 For every kind of beasts, and of birds, and of serpents, and of things in the sea, is tamed, and hath been tamed of mankind".*

THE BODY OF ADAM AND EVE

Adam and Eve were full of spiritual light. They were flesh and bone before they fell: "And the Lord God formed man of the dust of the, and breathed into his nostrils the breath of life and man became a living soul."

Genesis 2:7,"*7 And the LORD God formed man of the dust of the ground, and breathed into his nostrils the breath of life; and man became a living soul."*

Life in the spirit, **Romans 8:2**:"*2 For the law of the Spirit of life in Christ Jesus hath made me free from the law of sin and death."*

The Spirit is life in **Romans 8:10**: "*10 And if Christ be in you, the body is dead because of sin; but the Spirit is life because of righteousness."*

Adam said, this is now bone of my bone and flesh of my flesh, in **Genesis 2:23**, "*23 And Adam said, this is now bone of my bones, and flesh of my flesh: she* *shall be called Woman, because she was taken out of Man."*

Let us follow the phrase "flesh and bone" through the Bible and see what we can see in the Old Testament.

OLD TESTAMENT FLESH AND BONE

Genesis 29:14, *"¹⁴ And Laban said to him, Surely, thou art my bone and my flesh. And he abodes with him the space of a month."*

2 Samuel 5:1, *"Then came all the tribes of Israel to David unto Hebron, and spake, saying, Behold, we are thy bone and thy flesh."*

With just these few verses, we see that there is a direct link between **Adam, the first man,** and **the future last Adam, Jesus Christ**. Jacob is the father of all the tribes of Israel.

In fact, his name becomes Israel. The people of Israel are God's chosen people, and are surely of the bloodline of Seth; the same bloodline that will bring the Messiah.

Both Jacob and David are mentioned in Christ's genealogy. These are sons of God. Let's really pin this down by looking into the New Testament, where we will just use two verses.

JESUS JUST FLESH AND BONE AFTER HIS RESURRECTION

Christ after his resurrection, speaking to his disciples:

Luke 24:39, "*39 Behold my hands and my feet, that it is I myself: handle me, and see; for a spirit hath not flesh and bones, as ye see me have.*"

Paul speaking to born-again Christians about Christ in **Ephesians 5:30:** "*30 For we are members of his body, of his flesh, and of his bones.*"

For we are members of his body, of his flesh and of his bones.

Wow, this tells us a great deal about what kind of body we will have in the Kingdom of God. Yet, one must be born again from above to inherit an eternal body made of flesh and bone. Isn't that exciting?

Heaven will be like the Garden of Eden, where we do have bodies of flesh and bone. So we are not just spirits, floating around on clouds?

Jesus Christ has reconciled back to God as a new creature.

2 Corinthians 5:17-21, "*[17] Therefore if any man be in Christ, he is a new creature: old things are passed away; behold, all things are become new.*

[18] And all things are of God, who hath reconciled us to himself by Jesus Christ, and hath given to us the ministry of reconciliation;

[19] To wit, that God was in Christ, reconciling the world unto himself, not imputing their trespasses unto them; and hath committed unto us the word of reconciliation

²⁰ Now then we are ambassadors for Christ, as though God did beseech you by us: we pray you in Christ's stead, be ye reconciled to God.

²¹ For he hath made him to be sin for us, who knew no sin; that we might be made the righteousness of God in him."

Colossians 1:14-19, *"¹⁴ In whom we have redemption through his blood, even the forgiveness of sins:*

¹⁵ Who is the image of the invisible God, the firstborn of every creature:

¹⁶ For by him were all things created, that are in heaven, and that are in earth, visible and invisible, whether they be thrones, or dominions, or principalities, or powers: all things were created by him, and for him:

¹⁷ And he is before all things, and by him all things consist.

¹⁸And he is the head of the body, the church: who is the beginning, the firstborn from the dead; that in all things he might have the preeminence.

¹⁹For it pleased the Father that in him should all fulness dwell".

Reconciliation in Christ, **Colossians 1:20-21:** *"²⁰And, having made peace through the blood of his cross, by him to reconcile all things unto himself; by him, I say, whether they be things in earth, or things in heaven.*

²¹And you, that were sometime alienated and enemies in your mind by wicked works, yet now hath he reconciled."

In **1 Corinthians 15:45-49,** the **first man, Adam,** was made a living soul: The **Last Adam** was made a quickening spirit.

1 Corinthians 15:45-49, *"⁴⁵And so it is written, the first man Adam was made a living soul; the last Adam was made a quickening spirit.*

⁴⁶ *Howbeit that was not first which is spiritual, but that which is natural; and afterward that which is spiritual.*

⁴⁷ *The first man is of the earth, earthy; the second man is the Lord from heaven.*

⁴⁸ *As is the earthy, such are they also that are earthy: and as is the heavenly, such are they also that are heavenly.*

⁴⁹ *And as we have borne the image of the earthy, we shall also bear the image of the heavenly."*

THE FALL OF MAN

Genesis 3:1-13: *"Now the serpent was more subtil than any beast of the field which the* Lord *God had made. And he said unto the woman, Yea, hath God said, Ye shall not eat of every tree of the garden?*

²And the woman said unto the serpent, we may eat of the fruit of the trees of the garden:

³But of the fruit of the tree which is in the midst of the garden, God hath said, Ye shall not eat of it, neither shall ye touch it, lest ye die.

⁴And the serpent said unto the woman, Ye shall not surely die:

⁵For God doth know that in the day ye eat thereof, then your eyes shall be opened, and ye shall be as gods, knowing good and evil.

⁶And when the woman saw that the tree was good for food, and that it was pleasant to the eyes, and a tree to be desired to make one wise, she took of the fruit thereof, and did eat, and gave also unto her husband with her; and he did eat.

⁷ And the eyes of them both were opened, and they knew that they were naked; and they sewed fig leaves together, and made themselves aprons.

⁸ And they heard the voice of the LORD God walking in the garden in the cool of the day: and Adam and his wife hid themselves from the presence of the LORD God amongst the trees of the garden.

⁹ And the LORD God called unto Adam, and said unto him, Where art thou?

¹⁰ And he said, I heard thy voice in the garden, and I was afraid, because I was naked; and I hid myself.

¹¹ And he said, who told thee that thou wast naked? Hast thou eaten of the tree, whereof I commanded thee that thou shouldest not eat?

¹² And the man said, the woman whom thou gavest to be with me, she gave me of the tree, and I did eat.

¹³ And the LORD God said unto the woman, what is this that thou hast done? And the woman said, the serpent beguiled me, and I did eat.

The first pair were happy in their companionship and believed that it would last forever. They knew nothing of the Heavens of old.

2 Peter 3:5, "*⁵ For this they willingly are ignorant of, that by the word of God the heavens were of old, and the earth standing out of the water and in the water*".

Neither **Adam nor Eve** knew that fallen beings were under the leadership of Satan, or that their happiness was to end in a "fall that would get them expulsion from the Garden of Delights", and that sooner or later they should taste of physical death.

Adam and Eve were in true obedience. True obedience is to obey without knowing why.

The purpose God had in allowing **Adam** to be tempted and to fall is revealed in the gospel, and man's free will.

Free will, **John 6:37:** "*37 All that the Father giveth me shall come to me; and him that cometh to me I will in no wise cast out.*"

John 3:16 "*For God so loved the world, that he gave his only begotten Son, that whosoever believeth in him should not perish, but have everlasting life.*"

John 1:12 "*But as many as received him, to them gave the power to become the sons of God, even to them that believe on his name*".

The last call of the Bible is a general call. Revelation 22:17: "*And the Spirit and the bride say, Come. And let him that heareth say, Come. And let him that is athirst come. And whosoever will, let him take the water of life freely.*"

THE TEMPTATION OF JESUS

The temptation and fall are revealed in the gospel.

Matthew 4:1-11, "*Then was Jesus led up of the Spirit into the wilderness to be tempted of the devil.*

*²**A**nd when he had fasted forty days and forty nights, he was afterward an hungred.*

*³**A**nd when the tempter came to him, he said, If thou be the Son of God, command that these stones be made bread.*

*⁴**B**ut he answered and said, it is written, Man shall not live by bread alone, but by every word that proceedeth out of the mouth of God.*

*⁵**T**hen the devil taketh him up into the holy city, and setteth him on a pinnacle of the temple,*

*⁶**A**nd saith unto him, if thou be the Son of God, cast thyself down: for it is written, He shall give his angels charge concerning thee: and in their hands* *they shall bear thee up, lest at any time thou dash thy foot against a stone.*

*⁷ **J**esus said unto him, it is written again, thou shalt not tempt the Lord thy God.*

*⁸ **A**gain, the devil taketh him up into an exceeding high mountain, and sheweth him all the kingdoms of the world, and the glory of them;*

*⁹ **A**nd saith unto him, all these things will I give thee, if thou wilt fall down and worship me.*

*¹⁰ **T**hen saith Jesus unto him, get thee hence, Satan: for it is written, thou shalt worship the Lord thy God, and him only shalt thou serve.*

*¹¹ **T**hen the devil leaveth him, and, behold, angels came and ministered unto him."*

Luke 4:1-13, *"And Jesus being full of the Holy Ghost returned from Jordan, and was led by the Spirit into the wilderness,*

*2 **B**eing forty days tempted of the devil. And in those days, he did eat nothing: and when they were ended, he afterward hungered.*

*3 **A**nd the devil said unto him, if thou be the Son of God, command this stone that it be made bread.*

*4 **A**nd Jesus answered him, saying, it is written, that man shall not live by bread alone, but by every word of God.*

*5 **A**nd the devil, taking him up into a high mountain, shewed unto him all the kingdoms of the world in a moment of time.*

*6 **A**nd the devil said unto him, all this power will I give thee, and the glory of them: for that is delivered unto me; and to whomsoever I will I give it.*

*7 **I**f thou therefore wilt worship me, all shall be thine.*

*8 **A**nd Jesus answered and said unto him, get thee behind me, Satan: for it is written, thou shalt worship the Lord thy God, and him only shalt thou serve.*

*⁹ **A**nd he brought him to Jerusalem, and set him on a pinnacle of the temple, and said unto him, if thou be the Son of God, cast thyself down from hence:*

*¹⁰ **F**or it is written, He shall give his angels charge over thee, to keep thee:*

*¹¹ **A**nd in their hands, they shall bear thee up, lest at any time thou dash thy foot against a stone.*

*¹² **A**nd Jesus answering said unto him, it is said, Thou shalt not tempt the Lord thy God.*

*¹³ **A**nd when the devil had ended all the temptation, he departed from him for a season."*

If God had not permitted the human race to be tested and to fall, the world would never have had the supreme spectacle of his forgiving love and redemptive grace, as revealed on calvary, **Colossians 1:20-21,22 Reconciliation in Christ.**

Colossians 1:20-22, *"²⁰ **A**nd, having made peace through the blood of his cross, by him to reconcile all* *things unto himself; by him, I say, whether they be things in earth, or things in heaven.*

21 *And you, that were sometime alienated and enemies in your mind by wicked works, yet now hath he reconciled*

22 *In the body of his flesh through death, to present you holy and unblameable and unreproveable in his sight".*

Observing **Eve's** longing glances at the **"Fruit"** of the tree, the serpent (**Satan**) opened the conversation by craftily asking, "Yea, hath God said ye shall not eat of every tree of the Garden?"

The subtlety of this question is seen in its suggestion that God did not love them, and that it was unfair and unkind to forbid them anything.

In her answer, Eve betrays her feeling toward God by adding to the prohibition, saying, "Neither shall ye touch it", as if God was afraid to trust her. She also altered the penalty from "Thou shalt surely die" to "lest ye die," thus expressing doubt as to the certainly of death. It is a dangerous thing to add to or subtract from God's word.

Revelation 22:18-19, "*18 For I testify unto every man that heareth the words of the prophecy of this book, if any man shall add unto these things, God shall add unto him the plagues that are written in this book:*

19 And if any man shall take away from the words of the book of this prophecy, God shall take away his part out of the book of life, and out of the holy city, and from the things which are written in this book."

The commencement of the fall was the "deceitful handling of the word of God".

2 Corinthians 4:2, "*2 But have renounced the hidden things of dishonesty, not walking in craftiness, nor handling the word of God deceitfully; but by manifestation of the truth commending ourselves to every man's conscience in the sight of God.*"

Satan was the creator of the "seed of doubt". It was deposited in the heart or mind of **Eve** by Satan's question, "Yea, hath God said?" This led **Eve** to question the love of God.

The human race has inherited this microbe of unbelief from **Eve**.

Men do not openly deny the goodness of God so much as they question the statements of the word of God.

Satan, having sown the "seed of doubt" and perceived that the poison was working, next declared that God was a liar by saying, "Yea shall not surely die."

John 8:44, *"Ye are of your father the devil, and the lusts of your father ye will do. He was a murderer from the beginning, and abode not in the truth, because there is no truth in him. When he speaketh a lie, he speaketh of his own: for he is a liar, and the father of it."*

This is the devil's lie and it has been incorporated into the religious systems of today that teach that man shall not be eternally punished.

Satan then impugned God's motive by declaring that God did not want them to have a knowledge of "good and evil", lest they become God's like himself.

John 10:34, "*34 Jesus answered them, is it not written in your law, I said, Ye are gods?*"

Psalm 82:6-8 "*6 I have said, Ye are gods; and all of you are children of the most High.*

7 But ye shall die like men, and fall like one of the princes.

8 Arise, O God, judge the earth: for thou shalt inherit all nations."

This appealed to **Eve's curiosity and ambition**, and stirred up a torrent of desire in her heart when she saw that the tree was good for food.

James 1:13-14, "*[13] Let no man say when he is tempted, I am tempted of God: for God cannot be tempted with evil, neither tempteth he any man: [14] But every man is tempted, when he is drawn away of his own lust, and enticed.*"

1 John 2:15-17 "*[15] Love not the world, neither the things that are in the world. If any man loves the world, the love of the Father is not in him.*

[16] For all that is in the world, the lust of the flesh, and the lust of the eyes, and the pride of life, is not of the Father, but is of the world.

[17] And the world passeth away, and the lust thereof: but he that doeth the will of God abideth forever."

The lust of the flesh, and pleasure of the eyes (the lust of the eyes), and desirables to make one wise (the pride of life).

Eve did not wait to consult her husband, but put forth her hand and plucked and ate the fruit, and the

days of her innocence were ended. When **Adam** appeared without contrition of heart, she in turn
tempted him and he, not willing to be separated from
her, also ate. The result was the ruin the human race.

The woman was deceived, but **Adam** was not deceived.

1 Timothy 2:13-14 *"13 For Adam was first
formed, then Eve. 14 And Adam was not deceived, but
the woman being deceived was in the transgression."*

THE CURSE OF MAN AND EARTH

Genesis 3:14-20

"**14** And the LORD God said unto the serpent, because thou hast done this, thou art cursed above all cattle, and above every beast of the field; upon thy belly shalt thou go, and dust shalt thou eat all the days of thy life:

15 And I will put enmity between thee and the woman, and between thy seed and her seed; it shall bruise thy head, and thou shalt bruise his heel.

16 Unto the woman he said, I will greatly multiply thy sorrow and thy conception; in sorrow thou shalt bring forth children; and thy desire shall be to thy husband, and he shall rule over thee.

17 And unto Adam he said, because thou hast hearkened unto the voice of thy wife, and hast eaten of the tree, of which I commanded thee, saying, thou *shalt not eat of it: cursed is the ground for thy sake; in sorrow shalt thou eat of it all the days of thy life;*

[18] Thorns also and thistles shall it bring forth to thee; and thou shalt eat the herb of the field;

[19] In the sweat of thy face shalt thou eat bread, till thou return unto the ground; for out of it wast thou taken: for dust thou art, and unto dust shalt thou return.

[20] And Adam called his wife's name Eve; because she was the mother of all living.

Adam and Eve were created "innocent". Innocence is not "righteousness". Innocence cannot become "righteous" until tested.

If **Adam** and **Eve** had stood the "test", they would have become "righteous", or holy. They failed and instead became Sinners.

Adam's sin was the transgression of the law that God laid down as to the eating of the fruit of the

Garden; and grace was revealed and exercised when **Adam and Eve** were spared the penalty of their sin.

In 1 John 3:4, "*⁴Whosoever committeth sin transgresseth also the law: for sin is the transgression of the law.*"

In the fall of Man, the triumph of Satan was complete. The first effect of the disobedience of Adam and Eve was self-consciousness: "they saw that they were naked".

The result of this knowledge led them to invent clothing made of "fig leaves". All living creatures are clothed by nature; fish have scales, birds have feathers, and beasts have hair or fur or wool. But man, among all God's creatures, is left without clothing, and is compelled to have recourse to artificial covering. Why is this? It is the result of sin.

Adam and Eve at first wore no clothing, nor did they need to. Their state of innocence made them unashamed.

Adam and Eve dreaded meeting God, and so hid themselves in the forest when the Lord God came down to take his usual walk in the Garden in the cool of the day.

Heretofore, they had looked forward to the daily visit of the Lord God, but now they feared facing him. Thus, sin makes cowards of us all. By questioning them, the Lord God got them to sit in judgment on their own conduct.

Adam blamed his fall on **Eve**, but she blamed her fall on the serpent. God patiently listened to them and gave them an opportunity to justify their conduct. Then He passed judgment on them, but to the serpent, He gave no opportunity for justification.

But he said in **Genesis 3:14-15,** "*14 And the Lord God said unto the serpent, because thou hast done this, thou art cursed above all cattle, and above every beast of the field; upon thy belly shalt thou go, and dust shalt thou eat all the days of thy life:*

15 And I will put enmity between thee and the woman, and between thy seed and her seed; it shall bruise thy head, and thou shalt bruise his heel."

In the expression "thy seed" (Satan's seed) we have a prophetic reference to the Antichrist who as Satan's seed is called in **2 Thessalonians 2:3** the son of perdition.

2 Thessalonians 2:3, *"Let no man deceive you by any means: for that day shall not come, except there comes a falling away first, and that man of sin be revealed, the son of perdition".*

The woman's curse was that she should lose her position as man's equal and become subject to her husband, Adam. **Genesis 3:16,** *"16 Unto the woman he said, I will greatly multiply thy sorrow and thy conception; in sorrow thou shalt bring forth children; and thy desire shall be to thy husband, and he shall rule over thee."*

THE CURSE OF ADAM

Genesis 3:17-19, "*17 And unto Adam he said, because thou hast hearkened unto the voice of thy wife, and hast eaten of the tree, of which I commanded thee, saying, thou shalt not eat of it: cursed is the ground for thy sake; in sorrow shalt thou eat of it all the days of thy life;*

18 Thorns also and thistles shall it bring forth to thee; and thou shalt eat the herb of the field;

19 In the sweat of thy face shalt thou eat bread, till thou return unto the ground; for out of it wast thou taken: for dust thou art, and unto dust shalt thou return."

Adam's sin caused the whole earth to be cursed: "Cursed is the ground for thy sake; in sorrow shalt thou eat of it all the days of thy life. Thorns also and thistles shall it bring forth to thee: and thou shalt eat the herb of the field".

In **Romans 8:20-23** the whole creation groaneth and travaileth in pain together until now, waiting for redemption of the Earth and our body.

Romans 8:20-23 "²⁰ *For the creature was made subject to vanity, not willingly, but by reason of him who hath subjected the same in hope,*

²¹ *Because the creature itself also shall be delivered from the bondage of corruption into the glorious liberty of the children of God.*

²² *For we know that the whole creation groaneth and travaileth in pain together until now.*

²³ *And not only they, but ourselves also, which have the first fruits of the Spirit, even we ourselves groan within ourselves, waiting for the adoption, to wit, the redemption of our body.*

Jesus Christ hath redeemed us from the curse of the Law sin and will redeem the Earth. This is shown in:

A) **Galatians 3:10-18,** "¹⁰ For as many as are of the works of the law are under the curse: for it is written, cursed is every one that continueth not in all things which are written in the book of the law to do them.

¹¹ But that no man is justified by the law in the sight of God, it is evident: for, the just shall live by faith.

¹² And the law is not of faith: but, the man that doeth them shall live in them.

¹³ Christ hath redeemed us from the curse of the law, being made a curse for us: for it is written, cursed is every one that hangeth on a tree:

¹⁴ That the blessing of Abraham might come on the Gentiles through Jesus Christ; that we might receive the promise of the Spirit through faith.

¹⁵ Brethren, I speak after the manner of men; Though it be but a man's covenant, yet if

it be confirmed, no man disannulleth, or addeth thereto.

¹⁶ Now to Abraham and his seed were the promises made. He saith not, and to seeds, as of many; but as of one, and to thy seed, which is Christ.

¹⁷ And this I say, that the covenant, that was confirmed before of God in Christ, the law, which was four hundred and thirty years after, cannot disannul, that it should make the promise of none effect.

¹⁸ For if the inheritance be of the law, it is no more of promise: but God gave it to Abraham by promise."

B) **Galatians 3:19-29** *"¹⁹ Wherefore then serveth the law? It was added because of transgressions, till the seed should come to whom the promise was made; and it was ordained by angels in the hand of a mediator.*

²⁰ Now a mediator is not a mediator of one, but God is one.

²¹ Is the law then against the promises of God? God forbid: for if there had been a law given which could have given life, verily righteousness should have been by the law.

²² But the scripture hath concluded all under sin, that the promise by faith of Jesus Christ might be given to them that believe.

²³ But before faith came, we were kept under the law, shut up unto the faith which should afterwards be revealed.

²⁴ Wherefore the law was our schoolmaster to bring us unto Christ, that we might be justified by faith.

²⁵ But after that faith is come, we are no longer under a schoolmaster.

²⁶ For ye are all the children of God by faith in Christ Jesus.

²⁷ *For as many of you as have been baptized into Christ have put on Christ.*

²⁸ *There is neither Jew nor Greek, there is neither bond nor free, there is neither male nor female: for ye are all one in Christ Jesus.*

²⁹ *And if ye be Christ's, then are ye Abraham's seed, and heirs according to the promise."*

C) **2 Peter 3:10,13** *"¹⁰ But the day of the Lord will come as a thief in the night; in the which the heavens shall pass away with a great noise, and the elements shall melt with fervent heat, the earth also and the works that are therein shall be burned up.*

¹³ Nevertheless we, according to his promise, look for new heavens and a new earth, wherein dwelleth righteousness."

GOD MADE A SACRIFICE FOR ADAM AND EVE'S SIN

Genesis 3:22-24 "*²² And the L*ORD* God said, Behold, the man is become as one of us, to know good and evil: and now, lest he put forth his hand, and take also of the tree of life, and eat, and live forever:*

*²³ Therefore the L*ORD* God sent him forth from the garden of Eden, to till the ground from whence he was taken*

²⁴ So he drove out the man; and he placed at the east of the garden of Eden Cherubims, and a flaming sword which turned every way, to keep the way of the tree of life.

Genesis 3:21 "*Unto Adam also and to his wife did the L*ORD* God make coats of skins, and clothed them.*"

Adam and Eve sinned, and grace was revealed and exercised when **Adam and Eve** were spared the penalty of their sin.

God provided a sacrificed raiment, a raiment that would typify the putting away of sin. So, we read in **Genesis 3:21,** *"Unto Adam and his wife did the Lord God made coats of skins and clothed them."*

The Bible says in the book of **Hebrews 9:22,** *"And almost all things are by the Law purged with blood; and without shedding of blood is no remission."*

God provided the first sacrifices for sin in the Garden in the killing of some innocent animals. These were probably lambs, and were a type of the lamb of God and proclaimed the great truth that sin can only be put away by the shedding of blood

Hebrews 9:22, *"And almost all things are by the Law purged with blood; and without shedding of blood is no remission."*

God promised the seed of the woman should bruise the serpent's head. It is a significant fact that the giver of this promise was himself the promise, Jesus Christ.

The seed of the woman and He who clothed **Adam** and **Eve** in skins was the Lord God, the second person of the trinity, who was to become the lamb of God.

His death on Calvary was thus foreshadowed by the slaying of the lambs, whose skins were needed to cover the nakedness of Adam and Eve.

It is probable that God explained to Adam and Eve the significance of a bloody sacrifice for sin.

Genesis 3:21, *"Unto Adam also and to his wife did the* LORD *God make coats of skins, and clothed them".*

But Adam is not mentioned in the scriptures as offering such a sacrifice. Yet in the eleventh chapter of Hebrews, the list of old testament worthies in **Hebrews 11:1-2,** it said:

Hebrews 11:1-2 *"Now faith is the substance of things hoped for, the evidence of things not seen.* **² For** *by it the elders obtained a good report."*

Now, the first person mentioned in **Hebrews 11:3** is Abel, Adam and Eve's son. God thus explained it to Adam and Eve, who told Abel, their son, how to give an excellent sacrifice.

Hebrews 11:3, *"Through faith we understand that the worlds were framed by the word of God, so that things which are seen were not made of things which do appear."*

Training Your Children

The bible said in **Proverbs 22:6,** *"Train up a child in the way He should go: and when he is old, he will not depart from it."*

Ephesians 6:4, *"And, ye fathers, provoke not your children to wrath: but bring them up in the nurture and admonition of the Lord."*

Genesis 18:19, *"For I know him, that he will command his children and his household after him, and they shall keep the way of the LORD, to do justice and* *judgment; that the LORD may bring upon Abraham that which he hath spoken of him."*

Deuteronomy 6:7, 11:19:

6:7, *"And thou shalt teach them diligently unto thy children, and shalt talk of them when thou sittest in thine house, and when thou walkest by the way, and when thou liest down, and when thou risest up."*

11:19, *"And ye shall teach them your children, speaking of them when thou sittest in thine house, and when thou walkest by the way, when thou liest down, and when thou risest up."*

Psalm 78:4, *"We will not hide them from their children, shewing to the generation to come the praises of the LORD, and his strength, and his wonderful works that he hath done."*

2 Timothy 3:15, *"And that from a child thou hast known the holy scriptures, which are able to make thee wise unto salvation through faith which is in Christ Jesus."*

We do know of at least two instances later in Genesis where Eve exhibited faith in God. In the first example, Eve believed that God was going to send her a promised child, referring to Cain:

Genesis 4:1 *"And Adam knew Eve his wife; and she conceived, and bare Cain, and said, I have gotten a man from the LORD."*

From this first passage, we see that Eve trusted in the promise of God to provide a child. However, tragically, Cain actually kills Abel and God expels him from the presence of Adam and Eve.

Genesis 4:12-16, *"12 When thou tillest the ground, it shall not henceforth yield unto thee her strength; a fugitive and a vagabond shalt thou be in the earth.*

13 And Cain said unto the LORD, my punishment is greater than I can bear.

14 Behold, thou hast driven me out this day from the face of the earth; and from thy face shall I be hid;

*and I shall be a fugitive and a vagabond in the earth;
and it shall come to pass, that every one that findeth
me shall slay me.*

*15 And the LORD said unto him, therefore whoso-
ever slayeth Cain, vengeance shall be taken on him
sevenfold. And the LORD set a mark upon Cain, lest
any finding him should kill him.*

*16 And Cain went out from the presence of
the LORD, and dwelt in the land of Nod, on the east of
Eden."*

Not only has Eve lost Abel, she has also lost her
first-born son Cain. Despite her dire circumstances,
Eve continues to trust in God to provide.

Adam had relations with his wife again, and she
gave birth to a son, and name him Seth (which means
"appointed"), for Eve said God has appointed me another offspring in place of Abel, for Cain killed him.

Genesis 4:25 *"And Adam knew his wife again;
and she bare a son, and called his name Seth: For*

*God, said she, hath appointed me another seed in-
stead of Abel, whom Cain slew."*

Again, Eve continues to rely on the promise of god, this time she actually receives the appointed child who did not cause the headache which Cain cause her.

EVE AS AN EXAMPLE OF FAITH

According to the Bible, humanity was always jus-tified (made right or saved) before God by faith. This is shown in **Genesis 15:6, Romans 4:1-11, Hebrews 11:1-40:**

Genesis 15:6, *"And he believed in the LORD; and he counted it to him for righteousness."*

Romans 4:1-11, *"What shall we say then that Abraham our father, as pertaining to the flesh, hath found?*

² For if Abraham were justified by works, he hath whereof to glory; but not before God.

3 For what saith the scripture? Abraham believed God, and it was counted unto him for righteousness.

4 Now to him that worketh is the reward not reckoned of grace, but of debt.

5 But to him that worketh not, but believeth on him that justifieth the ungodly, his faith is counted for righteousness.

6 Even as David also describeth the blessedness of the man, unto whom God imputeth righteousness without works,

7 Saying, blessed are they whose iniquities are forgiven, and whose sins are covered.

8 Blessed is the man to whom the Lord will not impute sin.

9 Cometh this blessedness then upon the circumcision only, or upon the uncircumcision also? for we say that faith was reckoned to Abraham for righteousness.

10 *How was it then reckoned? when he was in cir-cumcision, or in uncircumcision? Not in circumcision, but in uncircumcision.*

11 *And he received the sign of circumcision, a seal of the righteousness of the faith which he had yet being uncircumcised: that he might be the father of all them that believe, though they be not circumcised; that righteousness might be imputed unto them also".*

Hebrews 11:1-40, *"Now faith is the substance of things hoped for, the evidence of things not seen.*

2 *For by it the elders obtained a good report.*

3 *Through faith we understand that the worlds were framed by the word of God, so that things which are seen were not made of things which do appear.*

4 *By faith Abel offered unto God a more excellent sacrifice than Cain, by which he obtained witness that he was righteous, God testifying of his gifts: and by it he being dead yet speaketh.*

⁵ By faith Enoch was translated that he should not see death; and was not found, because God had translated him: for before his translation he had this testimony, that he pleased God.

⁶ But without faith it is impossible to please him: for he that cometh to God must believe that he is, and that he is a rewarder of them that diligently seek him.

⁷ By faith Noah, being warned of God of things not seen as yet, moved with fear, prepared an ark to the saving of his house; by the which he condemned the world, and became heir of the righteousness which is by faith.

⁸ By faith Abraham, when he was called to go out into a place which he should after receive for an inheritance, obeyed; and he went out, not knowing whither he went.

⁹ By faith he sojourned in the land of promise, as in a strange country, dwelling in tabernacles with Isaac and Jacob, the heirs with him of the same promise:

¹⁰ For he looked for a city which hath foundations, whose builder and maker are God.

¹¹ Through faith also Sara herself received strength to conceive seed, and was delivered of a child when she was past age, because she judged him faithful who had promised.

¹² Therefore sprang there even of one, and him as good as dead, so many as the stars of the sky in multitude, and as the sand which is by the sea shore innumerable.

¹³ These all died in faith, not having received the promises, but having seen them afar off, and were persuaded of them, and embraced them, and confessed that they were strangers and pilgrims on the earth.

¹⁴ For they that say such things declare plainly that they seek a country.

15 And truly, if they had been mindful of that country from whence, they came out, they might have had opportunity to have returned.

16 But now they desire a better country, that is, a heavenly: wherefore God is not ashamed to be called their God: for he hath prepared for them a city.

17 By faith Abraham, when he was tried, offered up Isaac: and he that had received the promises offered up his only begotten son,

18 Of whom it was said, that in Isaac shall thy seed be called:

19 Accounting that God was able to raise him up, even from the dead; from whence also he received him in a figure.

20 By faith Isaac blessed Jacob and Esau concerning things to come.

21 By faith Jacob, when he was a dying, blessed both the sons of Joseph; and worshipped, leaning upon the top of his staff.

22 By faith Joseph, when he died, made mention of the departing of the children of Israel; and gave commandment concerning his bones.

23 By faith Moses, when he was born, was hid three months of his parents, because they saw he was a proper child; and they were not afraid of the king's commandment.

24 By faith Moses, when he was come to years, refused to be called the son of Pharaoh's daughter;

25 Choosing rather to suffer affliction with the people of God, than to enjoy the pleasures of sin for a season;

26 Esteeming the reproach of Christ greater riches than the treasures in Egypt: for he had respect unto the recompence of the reward.

27 By faith he forsook Egypt, not fearing the wrath of the king: for he endured, as seeing him who is invisible.

28 *Through faith he kept the passover, and the sprinkling of blood, lest he that destroyed the firstborn should touch them.*

29 *By faith they passed through the Red sea as by dry land: which the Egyptians assaying to do were drowned.*

30 *By faith the walls of Jericho fell down, after they were compassed about seven days.*

31 *By faith the harlot Rahab perished not with them that believed not, when she had received the spies with peace.*

32 *And what shall I more say? for the time would fail me to tell of Gedeon, and of Barak, and of Samson, and of Jephthae; of David also, and Samuel, and of the prophets:*

33 *Who through faith subdued kingdoms, wrought righteousness, obtained promises, stopped the mouths of lions.*

34 Quenched the violence of fire, escaped the edge of the sword, out of weakness were made strong, waxed valiant in fight, turned to fight the armies of the aliens.

35 Women received their dead raised to life again: and others were tortured, not accepting deliverance; that they might obtain a better resurrection:

36 And others had trial of cruel mockings and scourgings, yea, moreover of bonds and imprisonment:

37 They were stoned, they were sawn asunder, were tempted, were slain with the sword: they wandered about in sheepskins and goatskins; being destitute, afflicted, tormented;

38 (Of whom the world was not worthy:) they wandered in deserts, and in mountains, and in dens and caves of the earth.

39 And these all, having obtained a good report through faith, received not the promise:

40 God having provided some better thing for us, that they without us should not be made perfect."

Therefore, since Eve trusted in the Lord, there is good reason to believe that she was saved, in spite of her initial failure in the Garden of Eden. (**Genesis 3:16,** *"Unto the woman he said, I will greatly multiply thy sorrow and thy conception; in sorrow thou shalt bring forth children; and thy desire shall be to thy husband, and he shall rule over thee".*).

Eve can certainly serve as a model of faith and trust as a result of her later actions of faith in the book of Genesis.

Genesis 4:1,25, *"1And Adam knew Eve his wife; and she conceived, and bare Cain, and said, I have gotten a man from the LORD.*

25And Adam knew his wife again; and she bare a son, and called his name Seth: For God, said she, hath appointed me another seed instead of Abel, whom Cain slew."

If Adam followed her wise example, which is likely since it was through him that Jesus came (***Luke 3:38,*** *"38 Which was the son of Enos, which was the son of Seth, which was the son of Adam, which was the son of God")* he would have been saved also.

Eve was saved (**Genesis 3:15,** *"15 And I will put enmity between thee and the woman, and between thy seed and her seed; it shall bruise thy head, and thou shalt bruise his heel.*) and thus the seed and Adam were saved too, in Jesus' name. Amen.

God made a sacrifice in the Garden. **Genesis 3:21,** *"21 Unto Adam also and to his wife did the* L*ord* *God make coats of skins, and clothed them."*

This is according to **Hebrews 9:22,** *"22 And almost all things are by the law purged with blood; and without shedding of blood is no remission."*

Hebrews 10:10, *"10 By the which will we are sanctified through the offering of the body of Jesus Christ once for all. "*

The Old Testament annual sacrifice was a prefigure of the sacrifice that Christ made on the cross. Once for all.

EXPULSION FROM THE GARDEN

Genesis 3:22-24, "*22 And the LORD God said, Behold, the man is become as one of us, to know good and evil: and now, lest he put forth his hand, and take also of the tree of life, and eat, and live forever:*

23 Therefore the LORD God sent him forth from the garden of Eden, to till the ground from whence he was taken.

24 So he drove out the man; and he placed at the east of the garden of Eden Cherubims, and a flaming sword which turned every way, to keep the way of the tree of life."

In mercy, God drove the guilty but forgiven pair from the Garden, lest they eat of the "tree of life" and be doomed to live forever in their sinful mortal bodies. Thus, the first dispensation ended in the failure of the human race under condemnation, and the whole earth cures.

Men claim that innocence and a perfect environment are safeguards against wrongdoing, but the catastrophe of Eden proves that is not true.

This dispensation extends from the "fall" to the flood. It lasted for 1656 years and was this dispensation of conscience.

It shows what man will do when guided only by his conscience. Adam and Eve had no conscience before the fall.

Conscience is a knowledge of good and evil, and this Adam and Eve did not have until they ate of the fruit of the forbidden tree.

Conscience may produce fear and remorse, but it will not keep men from doing wrong, for conscience imparts no power.

So, God explained to Adam and Eve the significance of a body sacrificed for sin.

Man is a trinity and is composed of body, soul, and spirit. **1 Thessalonians 5:23,** "*²³ And the very God* *of peace sanctify you wholly; and I pray God your whole spirit and soul and body be preserved blameless unto the coming of our Lord Jesus Christ."*

THE THREEFOLD NATURE OF MAN

The **outer** is the **body of Man;** the **middle of man** is the **soul;** and the **inner part** is **the spirit** or **the carnal.**

Corinthians 3:1-3 *"And I, brethren, could not speak unto you as unto spiritual, but as unto carnal, even as unto babes in Christ.*

2 I have fed you with milk, and not with meat: for hitherto ye were not able to bear it, neither yet now are ye able.

3 For ye are yet carnal: for whereas there is among you envying, and strife, and divisions, are ye not carnal, and walk as men?"

The natural in **1 Corinthians 2:14** and the Spiritual in **1 Corinthians 3:1** were part of Man.

1 Corinthians 2:14, "*¹⁴ But the natural man re-ceiveth not the things of the Spirit of God: for they are foolishness unto him: neither can he know them, because they are spiritually discerned.*

1 Corinthians 3:1, "And I, brethren, could not speak unto you as unto spiritual, but as unto carnal, even as unto babes in Christ."

The body is the material world through the five senses: **1. Sight, 2. Smell, 3. Hearing, 4. Taste, and 5. Touch.**

In **1 Corinthians 2:14**, **Galatians 5:16-17**, **Romans 10:17:**

Galatians 5:16-17

"*¹⁶ This I say then, walk in the Spirit, and ye shall not fulfil the lust of the flesh.*

¹⁷ For the flesh lusteth against the Spirit, and the Spirit against the flesh: and these are contrary the one to the other: so that ye cannot do the things that ye would."

Romans 10:17

"*17 So then faith cometh by hearing, and hearing by the word of God.*

The gates to the Soul** **are 1. Imagination 2. Conscience 3. Memory 4. Reason 5. Affections"

Bible verses

Imagination: 1 Chronicles 28:9, 2 Corinthians 10:4-5.

Conscience: 1 Timothy 4:1-2, Titus 1:15

Reason: Isaiah 1:18-19, Acts 17:2

Memory: Proverbs 10:7, John 14:26, 1 Corinthians 15:2

Affections: Philippians 1:8, Philippians 2:1

Imagination:

1 Chronicles 28:9, "*9 And thou, Solomon my son, know thou the God of thy father, and serve* *him with a perfect heart and with a willing mind: for the* L_{ORD} *searcheth all hearts, and understandeth all the imaginations of the thoughts: if thou seek him, he will be found of thee; but if thou forsake him, he will cast thee off forever.*

2 Corinthians 10:4-5, *"For the weapons of our warfare are not carnal, but mighty through God to the pulling down of strong holds.*

⁵ Casting down imaginations, and every high thing that exalteth itself against the knowledge of God, and bringing into captivity every thought to the obedience of Christ;

Conscience:

1 Timothy 4:1-2, *"Now the Spirit speaketh expressly, that in the latter times some shall depart from the faith, giving heed to seducing spirits, and doctrines of devils;*

² Speaking lies in hypocrisy; having their conscience seared with a hot iron;"

Titus 1:15, "*15 Unto the pure all things are pure: but unto them that are defiled and unbe-lieving is nothing pure; but even their mind and conscience is defiled.*"

Reason:

Isaiah 1:18-19, "*18 Come now, and let us rea-son together, saith the LORD: though your sins be as scarlet, they shall be as white as snow; though they be red like crimson, they shall be as wool.*

19 If ye be willing and obedient, ye shall eat the good of the land".

Acts 17:2, "*2 And Paul, as his manner was, went in unto them, and three sabbath days rea-soned with them out of the scriptures*".

Memory:

Proverbs 10:7, "*7 The **memory** of the just is blessed: but the name of the wicked shall rot.*"

John 14:26, "*26 But the Comforter, which is the Holy Ghost, whom the Father will send in my name, he shall teach you all things, and bring all things to your remembrance, whatsoever I have said unto you."*

1 Corinthians 15:2, "*2 By which also ye are saved, if ye keep in* **memory** *what I preached unto you, unless ye have believed in vain."*

Affections:

Philippians 1:8, "*8 For God is my witness, how greatly I long for you all with the* **affection** *of Jesus Christ."*

Philippians 2:1, "*Therefore if there is any consolation in Christ, if any comfort of love, if any fellowship of the Spirit, if any* **affection** *and mercy".*

<u>**_The gates of the Spirit are_**</u>:

1. Faith

2. Hope

3. Reverence

4. Prayer

5. Worship

Faith: **1 Corinthians 13:13,** _"[13] And now abideth faith, hope, charity, these three; but the greatest of these is charity."_

Hope: **Hebrews 11:1,** _"Now faith is the substance of things hoped for, the evidence of things not seen., 6:19 Which hope we have as an anchor of the soul, both sure and steadfast, and which entereth into that within the veil"._

Reverence: **Hebrews 12:28,** _"Wherefore we receiving a kingdom which cannot be moved, let us have grace, whereby we may serve God acceptably with reverence and godly fear"._

Ephesians 5:33, *"Nevertheless let every one of you in particular so love his wife even as himself; and the wife see that she reverences her husband."*

Prayer: **Matthew 6:9-13,** *"⁹After this manner therefore pray ye: Our Father which art in heaven, Hallowed be thy name.¹⁰Thy kingdom come, thy will be done in earth, as it is in heaven.¹¹Give us this day our daily bread.¹²And forgive us our debts, as we forgive our debtors.¹³And lead us not into temptation, but deliver us from evil: For thine is the kingdom, and the power, and the glory, forever. Amen."*

Worship: **John 4:23,** *"But the hour cometh, and now is, when the true worshippers shall worship the Father in spirit and in truth: for the Father seeketh such to worship him."*

Psalm 96:9, *"O worship the L*ORD* in the beauty of holiness: fear before him, all the earth.*

ADAM AND EVE BARE CAIN

Genesis 4:1-2, *"And Adam knew Eve his wife; and she conceived, and bare Cain, and said, I have gotten a man from the LORD.*

²And she again bares his brother Abel. And Abel was a keeper of sheep, but Cain was a tiller of the ground."

Adam and Eve had no children before the Fall, but they were created for that purpose. This is clear from the words God spoke to them after their creation, when He blessed them.

God said in **Genesis 1:28,** *"And God blessed them, and God said unto them, be fruitful, and multiply, and replenish the earth, and subdue it: and have dominion over the fish of the sea, and over the fowl of the air, and over every living thing that moveth upon the earth. Be fruitful and replenish the Earth."*

In the words "Replenish the Earth" we see the evidence that people had been on Earth before it was thrown into a chaotic condition, and that its inhabitants in some way had been destroyed.

2 Peter 3:5-6, "*⁵For this they willingly are ignorant of, that by the word of God the heavens were of old, and the earth standing out of the water and in the water:*

⁶Whereby the world that then was, being overflowed with water, perished".

Isaiah 45:18, "*For thus saith the L*ᴏʀᴅ *that created the heavens; God himself that formed the earth and made it; he hath established it, he created it not in vain, he formed it to be inhabited: I am the L*ᴏʀᴅ; *and there is none else.*"

It does not follow, however, that those inhabitants were human beings like ourselves. No human remains have been found antedating the creation of man.

Right after the expulsion from the Garden, the first child was born to Adam and Eve was Cain a son. Cain was an agriculturist and the possession of large estate. Abel was a keeper of sheep. Not his father's, but his own. He was a grown man and a cattle owner.

Cain killed Abel when they were about 100 years old. The death of Abel was probably due to a religious dispute between Cain and Abel on the merit of religious offerings.

Abel claimed that a "bloody" sacrifice was necessary. Cain claimed that an offering of work taken from the soil which God had cursed was sufficient.

They put the matter to a test. God accepted Abel's offering and rejected Cain's offering. God then gave Cain a chance to bring a second offering—the God of a second chance. God reminded Cain that there was still time to bring a "sin offering."

Genesis 4:7, *"If thou doest well, shalt thou not be accepted? and if thou doest not well, sin lieth at* *the door. And unto thee shall be his desire, and thou shalt rule over him."*

The expression "sin lieth at the door", from **Genesis 4:7**, may be translated as "sin offering lieth at the door". But Cain would not listen, and nursed his anger for a long time.

Proverb 17:17 speaks of this adversity: "[17] A friend loveth at all times, and a brother is born for adversity."

The Bible says in **Ephesians 4:26,** *"Be ye angry, and sin not: let not the sun go down upon your wrath".*

And **Ephesians 4:27** says, *"Neither give place to the Devil."*

One day, while alone in the field with his brother, Cain brought the subject up again, for we read that Cain talked with Abel about the matter.

Genesis 4:8, *"And Cain talked with Abel his brother: and it came to pass, when they were in the* field, that Cain rose up against Abel his brother, and slew him."

The whole thing was a scheme of Satan's to destroy Abel, through whom the promised seed was to come.

The Bible said in **John 8:44,** *"Ye are of your father the devil, and the lusts of your father ye will do. He was a murderer from the beginning, and abode not in the truth, because there is no truth in him. When he speaketh a lie, he speaketh of his own: for he is a liar, and the father of it."*

Abel was childless, or at least did not have a son to succeed him. This is clear from the fact that Seth took his place.

Genesis 5:4, *"And the days of Adam after he had begotten Seth were eight hundred years: and he begat sons and daughters".*

Satan was not only the instigator of Abel's murder, he was the author of Cain's religion, spoken of by **Jude 1:11** as "the way of Cain":

Jude 1:11, *"Woe unto them! for they have gone in the way of Cain, and ran greedily after the error of Balaam for reward, and perished in the gainsaying of Core."*

Satan, the devil, had the power of death.

Hebrews 2:14, *"14 Forasmuch then as the children are partakers of flesh and blood, he also himself likewise took part of the same; that through death he might destroy him that had the power of death, that is, the devil".*

CAIN AND ABEL BROUGHT A SACRIFICE

Genesis 4:3-7, "³*And in process of time it came to pass, that Cain brought of the fruit of the ground an offering unto the LORD.*

⁴*And Abel, he also brought of the firstlings of his flock and of the fat thereof. And the LORD had respect unto Abel and to his offering:*

⁵*But unto Cain and to his offering he had not respect. And Cain was very wroth, and his countenance fell.*

⁶*And the LORD said unto Cain, why art thou wroth? and why is thy countenance fallen?*

⁷*If thou doest well, shalt thou not be accepted? and if thou doest not well, sin lieth at the door. And unto thee shall be his desire, and thou shalt rule over him.*"

God made the first sacrifice for sin in the Garden.

Genesis 3:21, *"Unto Adam also and to his wife did the LORD God make coats of skins, and clothed them."*

Thus, according to **Genesis 3:21,** unto Adam also and to his wife did the Lord God make coats of skins, and clothed them. Adam and Eve could only be secured by the killing of innocent animals, probably lambs, and were a type of the lamb of God. The great truth is that sin can only be put away by the shedding of blood.

Hebrews 9:22, *"And almost all things are by the law purged with blood: and without shedding of blood is no remission."*

We are not to understand that there was no "Law" before Moses or no "Grace" before Jesus Christ, for "Sin" is the "Transgression of the Law":

1 John 3:4, *"Whosoever committeth sin trans-gresseth also the law: for sin is the transgression of the law."*

Adam's sin, too, was the transgression of the law that God laid down as to the eating of the fruit of the Garden, and grace was revealed and exercised when Adam and Eve were spared the penalty of their sin.

So, we can say that Adam and Eve learned how to sacrifice from God, and Cain and Abel learned from their father and mother, Adam and Eve.

THE LAW OF SIN OFFERINGS

In **Leviticus 4:1-12,** it says, *"And the LORD spake unto Moses, saying, ² Speak unto the children of Israel, saying, if a soul shall sin through ignorance against any of the commandments of the LORD concerning things which ought not to be done, and shall do against any of them:*

³*If the priest that is anointed do sin according to the sin of the people; then let him bring for his sin, which he hath sinned, a young bullock without blemish unto the LORD for a sin offering.*

⁴*And he shall bring the bullock unto the door of the tabernacle of the congregation before the LORD; and shall lay his hand upon the bullock's head, and kill the bullock before the LORD.*

⁵*And the priest that is anointed shall take of the bullock's blood, and bring it to the tabernacle of the congregation:*

⁶*And the priest shall dip his finger in the blood, and sprinkle of the blood seven times before the LORD, before the vail of the sanctuary.*

⁷*And the priest shall put some of the blood upon the horns of the altar of sweet incense before the LORD, which is in the tabernacle of the congregation; and shall pour all the blood of the bullock at the bottom of the altar of the burnt offering, which is at the door of the tabernacle of the congregation.*

8 And he shall take off from it all the fat of the bull-ock for the sin offering; the fat that covereth the inwards, and all the fat that is upon the inwards,

9 And the two kidneys, and the fat that is upon them, which is by the flanks, and the caul above the liver, with the kidneys, it shall he take away,

10 As it was taken off from the bullock of the sacrifice of peace offerings: and the priest shall burn them upon the altar of the burnt offering.

11 And the skin of the bullock, and all his flesh, with his head, and with his legs, and his inwards, and his dung,

12 Even the whole bullock shall he carry forth without the camp unto a clean place, where the ashes are poured out, and burn him on the wood with fire: where the ashes are poured out shall he be burnt."

And the Lord spoke unto Moses in **Numbers 18:17-19,** saying, *"17 But the firstling of a cow, or the firstling of a sheep, or the firstling of a goat, thou shalt* not redeem; they are holy: thou shalt sprinkle their blood upon the altar, and shalt burn their fat for an offering made by fire, for a sweet savour unto the LORD.

[18] And the flesh of them shall be thine, as the wave breast and as the right shoulder are thine.

[19] All the heave offerings of the holy things, which the children of Israel offer unto the LORD, have I given thee, and thy sons and thy daughters with thee, by a statute forever: it is a covenant of salt for ever before the LORD unto thee and to thy seed with thee."

CONSECRATION OF FIRSTLING

Deuteronomy 15:19-22, "[19] All the firstling males that come of thy herd and of thy flock thou shalt sanctify unto the LORD thy God: thou shalt do no work with the firstling of thy bullock, nor shear the firstling of thy sheep.

²⁰ *Thou shalt eat it before the* L ORD *thy God year by year in the place which the* L ORD *shall choose, thou and thy household.*

²¹ *And if there be any blemish therein, as if it be lame, or blind, or have any ill blemish, thou shalt not sacrifice it unto the* L ORD *thy God.*

²² *Thou shalt eat it within thy gates: the unclean and the clean person shall eat it alike, as the roebuck, and as the hart."*

In the bible, the word of God tells us to train up a child:

Proverb 22:6, "⁶ *Train up a child in the way he should go: and when he is old, he will not depart from it."*

Ephesians 6:4, "⁴ *And, ye fathers, provoke not your children to wrath: but bring them up in the nurture and admonition of the Lord."*

Genesis 19:19, "¹⁹ *Behold now, thy servant hath found grace in thy sight, and thou hast magnified thy* *mercy, which thou hast shewed unto me in saving my life; and I cannot escape to the mountain, lest some evil take me, and I die".*

Deuteronomy 6:7-9, *"⁷ And thou shalt teach them diligently unto thy children, and shalt talk of them when thou sittest in thine house, and when thou walkest by the way, and when thou liest down, and when thou risest up.*

⁸ And thou shalt bind them for a sign upon thine hand, and they shall be as frontlets between thine eyes.

⁹ And thou shalt write them upon the posts of thy house, and on thy gates."

Deuteronomy 11:19, *"¹⁹ And ye shall teach them your children, speaking of them when thou sittest in thine house, and when thou walkest by the way, when thou liest down, and when thou risest up."*

Abel was a keeper of his own sheep, not his father's,. He was a grown man and a cattle owner.

Cain was an agriculturist and the possessor of large estates.

The Bible says in **Genesis 4:2,** *"And she again bares his brother Abel and Abel was a keeper of sheep, but Cain was a tiller of the ground."*

Genesis 4:3, *"And in process of time it came to pass, that Cain brought of the fruit of the ground an offering unto the Lord."*

Genesis 4:4, *"And Abel, he also brought of the firstling of his flock and of the fat thereof. And the Lord had respect unto Abel and to his offering."*

The death of Abel was probably due to a religions dispute between Cain and Abel on the merits of religious offerings.

Abel claimed that a "bloody" sacrifice was necessary. Cain claimed that an offering of "work" taken from the soil which God had cursed was sufficient. They put the matter to a test. God accepted Abel's offering and rejected Cain's offering.

THE CONTEST ON MOUNT CARMEL

The bible tells us in **1 Kings 18:21-40,** "*²¹ And Elijah came unto all the people, and said, how long halt ye between two opinions? if the LORD be God, follow him: but if Baal, then follow him. And the people answered him not a word.*

²² Then said Elijah unto the people, I, even I only, remain a prophet of the LORD; but Baal's prophets are four hundred and fifty men.

²³ Let them therefore give us two bullocks; and let them choose one bullock for themselves, and cut it in pieces, and lay it on wood, and put no fire under: and I will dress the other bullock, and lay it on wood, and put no fire under:

²⁴ And call ye on the name of your gods, and I will call on the name of the LORD: and the God that answereth by fire, let him be God. And all the people answered and said, it is well spoken.

25 And Elijah said unto the prophets of Baal, choose you one bullock for yourselves, and dress it first; for ye are many; and call on the name of your gods, but put no fire under.

26 And they took the bullock which was given them, and they dressed it, and called on the name of Baal from morning even until noon, saying, O Baal, hear us. But there was no voice, nor any that answered. And they leaped upon the altar which was made.

27 And it came to pass at noon, that Elijah mocked them, and said, cry aloud: for he is a god; either he is talking, or he is pursuing, or he is in a journey, or peradventure he sleepeth, and must be awaked.

28 And they cried aloud, and cut themselves after their manner with knives and lancets, till the blood gushed out upon them.

29 And it came to pass, when midday was past, and they prophesied until the time of the offering of the evening sacrifice, that there was neither voice, nor any to answer, nor any that regarded.

³⁰ And Elijah said unto all the people, Come near unto me. And all the people came near unto him. And he repaired the altar of the LORD that was broken down.

³¹ And Elijah took twelve stones, according to the number of the tribes of the sons of Jacob, unto whom the word of the LORD came, saying, Israel shall be thy name:

³² And with the stones he built an altar in the name of the LORD: and he made a trench about the altar, as great as would contain two measures of seed.

³³ And he put the wood in order, and cut the bullock in pieces, and laid him on the wood, and said, fill four barrels with water, and pour it on the burnt sacrifice, and on the wood.

³⁴ And he said, Do it the second time. And they did it the second time. And he said, Do it the third time. And they did it the third time. ³⁵ And the water ran round about the altar; and he filled the trench also with water.

36 And it came to pass at the time of the offering of the evening sacrifice, that Elijah the prophet came near, and said, LORD God of Abraham, Isaac, and of Israel, let it be known this day that thou art God in Israel, and that I am thy servant, and that I have done all these things at thy word.

37 Hear me, O LORD, hear me, that this people may know that thou art the LORD God, and that thou hast turned their heart back again.

38 Then the fire of the LORD fell, and consumed the burnt sacrifice, and the wood, and the stones, and the dust, and licked up the water that was in the trench.

39 And when all the people saw it, they fell on their faces: and they said, The LORD, he is the God; the LORD, he is the God.

40 And Elijah said unto them, Take the prophets of Baal; let not one of them escape. And they took them: and Elijah brought them down to the brook Kishon, and slew them there."

Also read **Numbers 16:1-50** for your convenience and understanding.

Because of the religious dispute, God always shows up and makes it plain that a sacrifice is so important to him. It must be done in God's way.

The Lord remonstrated with Cain and reminded him that there was still time to bring a "sin offering".

The expression "Sin lieth at the door" from **Genesis 4:7** may be translated as, "Sin offering lieth at the door", but Cain would not listen and nursed his anger.

Ephesians 4:26, *"Be ye angry, and sin not: let not the sun go down upon your wrath."*

Ephesians 4:27 *"Neither give place to the devil."*

Genesis 4:8, *"And Cain talked with Abel his brother and it came to pass when they were in the field that Cain rose up against Abel his brother and slew him."*

Genesis 4:9, *"And the Lord said unto Cain, where is Able the brother? And he said I know not: Am I my brother's keeper?"*

The whole thing was a scheme of Satan's to destroy Abel, through whom the "promised seed was to come".

Satan was not only the instigator of Abel's murder; he was the author of Cain's religion, spoken of by Jude as the way of Cain:

Jude 1:11, *"11 Woe unto them! for they have gone in the way of Cain, and ran greedily after the error of Balaam for reward, and perished in the gainsaying of Core."*

Satan was a murderer from the beginning, and above all, not in the truth.

John 8:44, *"44 Ye are of your father the devil, and the lusts of your father ye will do. He was a murderer from the beginning, and abode not in the truth, because there is no truth in him. When he speaketh a* lie, he speaketh of his own: for he is a liar, and the father of it."

1 John 3:15, "¹⁵ Whosoever hateth his brother is a murderer: and ye know that no murderer hath eternal life abiding in him."

Matthew 13:38, "³⁸ The field is the world; the good seed are the children of the kingdom; but the tares are the children of the wicked one".

1 John 2:15-17, "¹⁵ Love not the world, neither the things that are in the world. If any man loves the world, the love of the Father is not in him.

¹⁶ For all that is in the world, the lust of the flesh, and the lust of the eyes, and the pride of life, is not of the Father, but is of the world.

¹⁷ And the world passeth away, and the lust thereof: but he that doeth the will of God abideth forever."

1 John 3:8-10, "⁸ He that committeth sin is of the devil; for the devil sinneth from the beginning. For this *purpose, the Son of God was manifested, that he might destroy the works of the devil.*

⁹ Whosoever is born of God doth not commit sin; for his seed remaineth in him: and he cannot sin, because he is born of God.

¹⁰ In this the children of God are manifest, and the children of the devil: whosoever doeth not righteousness is not of God, neither he that loveth not his brother."

THE RESURRECTION OF JESUS CHRIST

The resurrection of Jesus is the foundation of fact on which Christianity is built.

1 Corinthians 15:17, *"17 And if Christ be not raised, your faith is vain; ye are yet in your sins."*

The proof of Jesus' "deity" depended on his resurrection from the dead. Five different times, he declared that he would be crucified and buried, and that on the third day he would rise from the dead.

Matthew 12:39-40, *"39 But he answered and said unto them, an evil and adulterous generation seeketh after a sign; and there shall no sign be given to it, but the sign of the prophet Jonas:*

40 For as Jonas was three days and three nights in the whale's belly; so, shall the Son of man be three days and three nights in the heart of the earth."

Matthew 2:17-19, "[17] *Then was fulfilled that which was spoken by Jeremiah the prophet, saying,*

[18] *In Rama was there a voice heard, lamentation, and weeping, and great mourning, Rachel weeping for her children, and would not be comforted, because they are not.*

[19] *But when Herod was dead, behold, an angel of the Lord appeareth in a dream to Joseph in Egypt".*

And shall deliver him to the Gentiles to mock, and to scourge, and to crucify him: And the third day he shall rise again.

Matthew 26:30-32, "[30] *And when they had sung a hymn, they went out into the mount of Olives.*

[31] *Then saith Jesus unto them, all ye shall be offended because of me this night: for it is written, I will smite the shepherd, and the sheep of the flock shall be scattered abroad.*

[32] *But after I am risen again, I will go before you into Galilee."*

Luke 18:31-33, "*31 Then he took unto him the twelve, and said unto them, Behold, we go up to Jerusalem, and all things that are written by the prophets concerning the Son of man shall be accomplished.*

32 For he shall be delivered unto the Gentiles, and shall be mocked, and spitefully entreated, and spitted on:

33 And they shall scourge him, and put him to death: and the third day he shall rise again."

Jesus answered the Jews:

John 2:19-22, "*19 Jesus answered and said unto them, destroy this temple, and in three days I will raise it up.*

20 Then said the Jews, Forty and six years was this temple in building, and wilt thou rear it up in three days?

21 But he spake of the temple of his body.

²² When therefore he was risen from the dead, his disciples remembered that he had said this unto them; and they believed the scripture, and the word which Jesus had said."

Destroy this temple, and in three days I will raise it up. He referred to the Temple of his body.

If He had not risen, we would not have known whether He was what He claimed to be or not, but the Apostle Paul said He was "declared" (demonstrated) to be the son of God by the resurrection from the dead.

Roman 1:4, *"⁴ And declared to be the Son of God with power, according to the spirit of holiness, by the resurrection from the dead".*

Jesus came to take the sinner's place and satisfy the law. If Jesus had not risen from the dead, we would not have known whether this had been done.

According to the scripture, Jesus' sentence was that he should remain in the grave three days, when the time was up, no power in heaven, earth, or hell could hold him there a minute longer.

In **Acts 2:24** we read, "*²⁴ Whom God hath raised up, having loosed the pains of death: because it was not possible that he should be holden of it.*"

Whom God raised up from the dead, having loosed the pains (power) of death because it was not possible that He should be holden of it.

In **Psalm 16:10** we read, "*For thou wilt not leave my soul in Hell; neither wilt thou suffer thine holy one to see corruption.*"

In **Acts 2:31,** "*³¹ He seeing this before spake of the resurrection of Christ, that his soul was not left in hell, neither his flesh did see corruption.*"

Therefore, Jesus had to rise before the fourth day, when corruption is supposed to set in. The resurrection of Jesus is proof that "Death" has been conquered.

When Jesus appeared to John on the Isle of Patmos, He declared, "I am He that liveth, and was dead: And behold I am alive for evermore, amen; and have the keys of 'Hell' (Hades, the underworld) and of 'Death' (The Grave)".

Revelation 1:18, "*¹⁸ I am he that liveth, and was dead; and, behold, I am alive for evermore, amen; and have the keys of hell and of death.*"

But it was not "Death" that had taken Christ captive. Christ simply pursued "Death" into his own dominions, and then, conquering him, came forth leading captivity captive and crying, "I am the resurrection and life."

John 11:25, "*²⁵ Jesus said unto her, I am the resurrection, and the life: he that believeth in me, though he were dead, yet shall he live*".

When Jesus rose from the dead, He "abolished death" and "brought life and immortality to light".

2 Timothy 1:10, *"¹⁰ But is now made manifest by the appearing of our Saviour Jesus Christ, who hath abolished death, and hath brought life and immortality to light through the gospel".*

That is, He took from death its terrors, and made provisions by which we shall be freed from bonds of death by the resurrection of our bodies, so that ultimately there will be no more death.

Revelation 21:4, *"⁴ And God shall wipe away all tears from their eyes; and there shall be no more death, neither sorrow, nor crying, neither shall there be any more pain: for the former things are passed away."*

Therefore, because the tomb could not hold Jesus, it shall not be able to hold us, for the spirit of him who raised up Jesus from the dead dwell in us. He that raised Christ from the dead shall quicken our mortal bodies by his spirit that dwelleth in us that is raise us from the dead.

Romans 8:11, *"11 But if the Spirit of him that raised up Jesus from the dead dwell in you, he that raised up Christ from the dead shall also quicken your mortal bodies by his Spirit that dwelleth in you."*

THE FACT OF THE RESURRECTION OF JESUS:

There can be no question as to Jesus' death on the cross.

All four Gospels, Matthew, Mark, Luke, and John, tell us that Jesus "Yielded up his spirit: Death did not conquer him. He yielded up his life of his own accord."

Jesus said, "I have power to lay down my life and I have power to take it again".

John 10:17-18, *"17 Therefore doth my Father love me, because I lay down my life, that I might take it again.*

18 No man taketh it from me, but I lay it down of myself. I have power to lay it down, and I have power to take it again. This commandment have I received of my Father."

The Roman soldiers did not break the bones of Jesus because they saw He was dead.

John 19:33, "*33 But when they came to Jesus, and saw that he was dead already, they brake not his legs*".

But when they came to Jesus, and saw that He was dead already, they brake not his legs: And the centurion testified to Pilate that Jesus was dead.

Mark 15:43-45, "*43 Joseph of Arimathaea, an honourable counsellor, which also waited for the kingdom of God, came, and went in boldly unto Pilate, and craved the body of Jesus.*

44 And Pilate marvelled if he were already dead: and calling unto him the centurion, he asked him whether he had been any while dead.

45 And when he knew it of the centurion, he gave the body to Joseph."

The most remarkable testimony to the physical resurrection of the body of Jesus is found in the statement of the Apostle.

John 20:6-7, "*⁶ Then cometh Simon Peter following him, and went into the sepulchre, and seeth the linen clothes lie,*

⁷ And the napkin, that was about his head, not lying with the linen clothes, but wrapped together in a place by itself."

Jesus arose. He just slipped out of his burial clothes, leaving them behind as a silent witness that his body was not stolen. For if his body had been stolen, the thieves would not have removed his grave clothes. And if they had for any reason, they would not have left them in order.

No one actually saw Jesus rise from the dead, but there were many witnesses who saw him after his resurrection, and not weeks and months after but the very day He arose.

When Jesus appeared to his disciples, he was in robust health and able to walk half a dozen miles to Emmaus with two of his disciples on the afternoon of the day He arose.

The miracle of Christ resurrection was twofold:

1. Restoration **to Life,** and

2. Restoration **to Health.**

On the day of his resurrection, Jesus appeared to his disciples five times.

First, He appeared to Mary Magdalene in **John 20:11-18:** "*11 But Mary stood without at the sepulchre weeping: and as she wept, she stooped down, and looked into the sepulchre,*

12 And seeth two angels in white sitting, the one at the head, and the other at the feet, where the body of Jesus had lain.

13 And they say unto her, Woman, why weepest thou? She saith unto them, because they have taken

away my L ORD*, and I know not where they have laid
him.*

*¹⁴ And when she had thus said, she turned herself
back, and saw Jesus standing, and knew not that it
was Jesus.*

*¹⁵ Jesus saith unto her, Woman, why weepest
thou? whom seekest thou? She, supposing him to be
the gardener, saith unto him, Sir, if thou have borne
him hence, tell me where thou hast laid him, and I will
take him away.*

*¹⁶ Jesus saith unto her, Mary. She turned herself,
and saith unto him, Rabboni; which is to say, Master.*

*¹⁷ Jesus saith unto her, touch me not; for I am not
yet ascended to my Father: but go to my brethren,
and say unto them, I ascend unto my Father, and your
Father; and to my God, and your God.*

*¹⁸ Mary Magdalene came and told the disciples that
she had seen the* L ORD*, and that he had spoken these
things unto her."*

Second, He appeared to the woman in **Matthew 28:9-10:** "*⁹ And as they went to tell his disciples, behold, Jesus met them, saying, All hail. And they came and held him by the feet, and worshipped him.*

¹⁰ Then said Jesus unto them, be not afraid: go tell my brethren that they go into Galilee, and there shall they see me."

Third, He appeared to Peter in **Luke 24:34:** "*³⁴ Saying, The Lord is risen indeed, and hath appeared to Simon.*"

Fourth, He appeared in the afternoon to the two disciples on the road to Emmaus:

Luke 24:13-35, "*¹³ And, behold, two of them went that same day to a village called Emmaus, which was from Jerusalem about threescore furlongs.*

¹⁴ And they talked together of all these things which had happened.

¹⁵ And it came to pass, that, while they communed together and reasoned, Jesus himself drew near, and went with them.

¹⁶ But their eyes were holden that they should not know him.

¹⁷ And he said unto them, what manner of communications are these that ye have one to another, as ye walk, and are sad?

¹⁸ And the one of them, whose name was Cleopas, answering said unto him, Art thou only a stranger in Jerusalem, and hast not known the things which are come to pass there in these days?

¹⁹ And he said unto them, What things? And they said unto him, Concerning Jesus of Nazareth, which was a prophet mighty in deed and word before God and all the people:

²⁰ And how the chief priests and our rulers delivered him to be condemned to death, and have crucified him.

²¹ But we trusted that it had been he which should have redeemed Israel: and beside all this, today is the third day since these things were done.

²² Yea, and certain women also of our company made us astonished, which were early at the sepulchre;

²³ And when they found not his body, they came, saying, that they had also seen a vision of angels, which said that he was alive.

²⁴ And certain of them which were with us went to the sepulchre, and found it even so as the women had said: but him they saw not.

²⁵ Then he said unto them, O fools, and slow of heart to believe all that the prophets have spoken:

²⁶ Ought not Christ to have suffered these things, and to enter into his glory?

²⁷ And beginning at Moses and all the prophets, he expounded unto them in all the scriptures the things concerning himself.

28 And they drew nigh unto the village, whither they went: and he made as though he would have gone further.

29 But they constrained him, saying, abide with us: for it is toward evening, and the day is far spent. And he went in to tarry with them.

30 And it came to pass, as he sat at meat with them, he took bread, and blessed it, and brake, and gave to them.

31 And their eyes were opened, and they knew him; and he vanished out of their sight.

32 And they said one to another, did not our heart burn within us, while he talked with us by the way, and while he opened to us the scriptures?

33 And they rose up the same hour, and returned to Jerusalem, and found the eleven gathered together, and them that were with them,

34 Saying, The Lord is risen indeed, and hath appeared to Simon.

35 And they told what things were done in the way, and how he was known of them in breaking of bread."

And fifth, He appeared in the evening to a number of the disciples in the upper room:

In **John 20:19,** *"19 Then the same day at evening, being the first day of the week, when the doors were shut where the disciples were assembled for fear of the Jews, came Jesus and stood in the midst, and saith unto them, Peace be unto you."*

Luke 24:36-48 *"36 And as they thus spake, Jesus himself stood in the midst of them, and saith unto them, Peace be unto you.*

37 But they were terrified and affrighted, and supposed that they had seen a spirit.

38 And he said unto them, why are ye troubled? and why do thoughts arise in your hearts?

39 Behold my hands and my feet, that it is I myself: handle me, and see; for a spirit hath not flesh and bones, as ye see me have.

⁴⁰ And when he had thus spoken, he shewed them his hands and his feet.

⁴¹ And while they yet believed not for joy, and wondered, he said unto them, Have ye here any meat?

⁴² And they gave him a piece of a broiled fish, and of an honeycomb.

⁴³ And he took it, and did eat before them.

⁴⁴ And he said unto them, these are the words which I spake unto you, while I was yet with you, that all things must be fulfilled, which were written in the law of Moses, and in the prophets, and in the psalms, concerning me.

⁴⁵ Then opened he their understanding, that they might understand the scriptures,

⁴⁶ And said unto them, thus it is written, and thus it behooved Christ to suffer, and to rise from the dead the third day:

⁴⁷ And that repentance and remission of sins should be preached in his name among all nations, beginning at Jerusalem.

⁴⁸ And ye are witnesses of these things."

A week later, in the same room, He again appeared to his disciples, Thomas being present:

In **John 20:24-29,** *"²⁴ But Thomas, one of the twelve, called Didymus, was not with them when Jesus came.*

²⁵ The other disciples therefore said unto him, we have seen the LORD. But he said unto them, Except I shall see in his hands the print of the nails, and put my finger into the print of the nails, and thrust my hand into his side, I will not believe.

²⁶ And after eight days again his disciples were within, and Thomas with them: then came Jesus, the doors being shut, and stood in the midst, and said, Peace be unto you.

²⁷ *Then saith he to Thomas, reach hither thy finger, and behold my hands; and reach hither thy hand, and thrust it into my side: and be not faithless, but believing.*

²⁸ *And Thomas answered and said unto him, My LORD and my God.*

²⁹ *Jesus saith unto him, Thomas, because thou hast seen me, thou hast believed: blessed are they that have not seen, and yet have believed."*

Later, He appeared to the "eleven disciples" on a mountain in Galilee:

In **Matthew 28:16-20,** "¹⁶ *Then the eleven disciples went away into Galilee, into a mountain where Jesus had appointed them.*

¹⁷ *And when they saw him, they worshipped him: but some doubted.*

¹⁸ *And Jesus came and spake unto them, saying, all power is given unto me in heaven and in earth.*

¹⁹ *Go ye therefore, and teach all nations, baptizing them in the name of the Father, and of the Son, and of the Holy Ghost:*

²⁰ *Teaching them to observe all things whatsoever I have commanded you: and, lo, I am with you always, even unto the end of the world. Amen."*

Mark 16:14-18, *"*¹⁴*Afterward he appeared unto the eleven as they sat at meat, and upbraided them with their unbelief and hardness of heart, because they believed not them which had seen him after he was risen.*

¹⁵ *And he said unto them, go ye into all the world, and preach the gospel to every creature.*

¹⁶ *He that believeth and is baptized shall be saved; but he that believeth not shall be damned.*

¹⁷ *And these signs shall follow them that believe; In my name shall they cast out devils; they shall speak with new tongues;*

18 They shall take up serpents; and if they drink any deadly thing, it shall not hurt them; they shall lay hands on the sick, and they shall recover."

Then He appeared to 500 Brethren at once:

In **1 Corinthians 15:6,** *"6 After that, he was seen of above five hundred brethren at once; of whom the greater part remains unto this present, but some are fallen asleep."*

Then to James:

In **1 Corinthians 15:7,** *"7 After that, he was seen of James; then of all the apostles."*

And then, forty days after his resurrection, He ascended to Heaven in the presence of his disciples from the mount of olives.

In **Acts 1:9-12,** *"9 And when he had spoken these things, while they beheld, he was taken up; and a cloud received him out of their sight.*

¹⁰ *And while they looked steadfastly toward heaven as he went up, behold, two men stood by them in white apparel;*

¹¹ *Which also said, Ye men of Galilee, why stand ye gazing up into heaven? this same Jesus, which is taken up from you into heaven, shall so come in like manner as ye have seen him go into heaven.*

¹² *Then returned they unto Jerusalem from the mount called Olivet, which is from Jerusalem a sabbath day's journey."*

THE BIBLE SPEAKS OF THREE KINDS OF RESURRECTION

1. NATIONAL RESURRECTION

This refers to Israel, who are now nationally dead and buried in the "Graveyard of the Nations", but who are to be revived and restored to their own land.

Hosea 6:1-2, *"Come, and let us return unto the LORD: for he hath torn, and he will heal us; he hath smitten, and he will bind us up.*

² After two days will he revive us: in the third day he will raise us up, and we shall live in his sight."

Isaiah 1:18, *"¹⁸ Come now, and let us reason together, saith the LORD: though your sins be as scarlet, they shall be as white as snow; though they be red like crimson, they shall be as wool. Come now, and let us reason together, said the Lord though your sins be as scarlet, they shall be as white as snow; though they be red like crimson, they shall be as wool."*

Deuteronomy 32:39, *"See now that I, even I, am he, and there is no God with me: I kill, and I make alive; I wound, and I heal: Neither is there any that can deliver out of my hand."*

Jeremiah 30:17-24 *"17 For I will restore health unto thee, and I will heal thee of thy wounds, saith the LORD; because they called thee an Outcast, saying, this is Zion, whom no man seeketh after.*

18 Thus saith the LORD; Behold, I will bring again the captivity of Jacob's tents, and have mercy on his dwelling places; and the city shall be builded upon her own heap, and the palace shall remain after the manner thereof.

19 And out of them shall proceed thanksgiving and the voice of them that make merry: and I will multiply them, and they shall not be few; I will also glorify them, and they shall not be small.

20 Their children also shall be as aforetime, and their congregation shall be established before me, and I will punish all that oppress them.

²¹ *And their nobles shall be of themselves, and their governor shall proceed from the midst of them; and I will cause him to draw near, and he shall approach unto me: for who is this that engaged his heart to approach unto me? saith the* Lord*.*

²² *And ye shall be my people, and I will be your God.*

²³ *Behold, the whirlwind of the* Lord *goeth forth with fury, a continuing whirlwind: it shall fall with pain upon the head of the wicked.*

²⁴ *The fierce anger of the* Lord *shall not return, until he hath done it, and until he has performed the intents of his heart: in the latter days ye shall consider it."*

1 Corinthians 15:4, *"And that he was buried, and that he rose again the third day according to the scriptures".*

THE RESTORATION OF ISRAEL AS A FACT

Amos 9:14-15, "[14] *And I will bring again the captivity of my people of Israel, and they shall build the waste cities, and inhabit them; and they shall plant vineyards, and drink the wine thereof; they shall also make gardens, and eat the fruit of them.*

[15] *And I will plant them upon their land, and they shall no more be pulled up out of their land which I have given them, saith the LORD thy God.*"

If you say this prophecy was fulfilled in the restoration from the "Babylonian Captivity", not so far—they were driven out of the land after that. This promise is that they shall no more be pulled up out of their land, and thus must refer to some future restoration.

The return from the Babylonian captivity was the first restoration, and the scripture speaks of a second.

Isaiah 11:11, "[11] *And it shall come to pass in that day, that the Lord shall set his hand again the second time to recover the remnant of his people, which shall* *be left, from Assyria, and from Egypt, and from Pathros, and from Cush, and from Elam, and from Shinar, and from Hamath, and from the islands of the sea."*

The Jews have only been restored once, and that was from Babylon.

The march from Egypt to Canaan was not a restoration. You cannot have anything restored to you unless it has been in your possession before, and Palestine was never in possession of the children of Israel until after its conquest by Joshua.

Again, the Jews are to come this time not from the East, as when they returned from the Babylonish captivity, but from the North and from all countries.

Jeremiah 16:14-15, *"¹⁴ Therefore, behold, the days come, saith the L*ORD*, that it shall no more be said, The L*ORD* liveth, that brought up the children of Israel out of the land of Egypt; ¹⁵ But, The L*ORD* liveth, that brought up the children of Israel from the land of the north, and from all the lands whither he had driven* them: and I will bring them again into their land that I gave unto their fathers."*

Also, in **Isaiah 43:5-7,** "*5 Fear not: for I am with thee: I will bring thy seed from the east, and gather thee from the west;*

6 I will say to the north, give up; and to the south, keep not back: bring my sons from far, and my daughters from the ends of the earth;

7 Even every one that is called by my name: for I have created him for my glory, I have formed him; yea, I have made him."

As to the time of Israel's restoration: it will happen when "the times of the Gentiles have been fulfilled".

Luke 21:24, "*24 And they shall fall by the edge of the sword, and shall be led away captive into all nations: and Jerusalem shall be trodden down of the Gentiles, until the times of the Gentiles be fulfilled."*

As to the manner: Gathered back, unconverted. Before conversion, they are to be judged.

1. **Ezekiel 36:24-27,** "²⁴ *For I will take you from among the heathen, and gather you out of all countries, and will bring you into your own land.*

   ²⁵ *Then will I sprinkle clean water upon you, and ye shall be clean: from all your filthiness, and from all your idols, will I cleanse you.*

   ²⁶ *A new heart also will I give you, and a new spirit will I put within you: and I will take away the stony heart out of your flesh, and I will give you a heart of flesh.*

   ²⁷ *And I will put my spirit within you, and cause you to walk in my statutes, and ye shall keep my judgments, and do them.*"

2. **Ezekiel 20:34-38,** "³⁴ *And I will bring you out from the people, and will gather you out of the countries wherein ye are scattered, with a mighty hand, and with a stretched-out arm, and with fury poured out.*

35 And I will bring you into the wilderness of the people, and there will I plead with you face to face.

36 Like as I pleaded with your fathers in the wilderness of the land of Egypt, so will I plead with you, saith the Lord God.

37 And I will cause you to pass under the rod, and I will bring you into the bond of the covenant:

38 And I will purge out from among you the rebels, and them that transgress against me: I will bring them forth out of the country where they sojourn, and they shall not enter into the land of Israel: and ye shall know that I am the Lord."

3. Ezekiel 22:19-22, *"19 Therefore thus saith the Lord God; Because ye are all become dross, behold, therefore I will gather you into the midst of Jerusalem.*

²⁰ *As they gather silver, and brass, and iron, and lead, and tin, into the midst of the furnace, to blow the fire upon it, to melt it; so, will I gather you in mine anger and in my fury, and I will leave you there, and melt you.*

²¹ *Yea, I will gather you, and blow upon you in the fire of my wrath, and ye shall be melted in the midst thereof.*

²² *As silver is melted in the midst of the furnace, so shall ye be melted in the midst thereof; and ye shall know that I the* LORD *have poured out my fury upon you."*

4. **Malachi 3:1-3,** *"Behold, I will send my messenger, and he shall prepare the way before me: and the* LORD*, whom ye seek, shall suddenly come to his temple, even the messenger of the covenant, whom ye delight in: behold, he shall come, saith the* LORD *of hosts.*

²But who may abide the day of his coming? and who shall stand when he appeareth? for he is like a refiner's fire, and like fullers' soap:

*³And he shall sit as a refiner and purifier of silver: and he shall purify the sons of Levi, and purge them as gold and silver, that they may offer unto the L*ORD *an offering in righteous-ness."*

5. Zechariah 14:1-11, *"Behold, the day of the L*ORD *cometh, and thy spoil shall be divided in the midst of thee.*

²For I will gather all nations against Jerusa-lem to battle; and the city shall be taken, and the houses rifled, and the women ravished; and half of the city shall go forth into captivity, and the residue of the people shall not be cut off from the city.

*³Then shall the L*ORD *go forth, and fight against those nations, as when he fought in the day of battle.*

⁴And his feet shall stand in that day upon the mount of Olives, which is before Jerusalem on the east, and the mount of Olives shall cleave in the midst thereof toward the east and toward the west, and there shall be a very great valley; and half of the mountain shall remove toward the north, and half of it toward the south.

⁵And ye shall flee to the valley of the mountains; for the valley of the mountains shall reach unto Azal: yea, ye shall flee, like as ye fled from before the earthquake in the days of Uzziah king of Judah: and the Lord my God shall come, and all the saints with thee.

⁶And it shall come to pass in that day, that the light shall not be clear, nor dark:

⁷But it shall be one day which shall be known to the Lord, not day, nor night: but it shall come to pass, that at evening time it shall be light.

⁸And it shall be in that day, that living waters shall go out from Jerusalem; half of them toward the former sea, and half of them toward the hinder sea: in summer and in winter shall it be.

⁹And the Lord *shall be king over all the earth: in that day shall there be one* Lord*, and his name one.*

¹⁰All the land shall be turned as a plain from Geba to Rimmon south of Jerusalem: and it shall be lifted up, and inhabited in her place, from Benjamin's gate unto the place of the first gate, unto the corner gate, and from the tower of Hananeel unto the king's winepresses.

¹¹And men shall dwell in it, and there shall be no more utter destruction; but Jerusalem shall be safely inhabited."

The Jews have never as yet had such an experience as this. It is spoken of in:

1. **Jeremiah 30:4-7:** "⁴*And these are the words that the* LORD *spake concerning Israel and concerning Judah.*

   ⁵*For thus saith the* LORD*; We have heard a voice of trembling, of fear, and not of peace.*

   ⁶*Ask ye now, and see whether a man doth travail with child? wherefore do I see every man with his hands on his loins, as a woman in travail, and all faces are turned into paleness?*

   ⁷*Alas! for that day is great, so that none is like it: it is even the time of Jacob's trouble, but he shall be saved out of it.*"

And in:

2. **Daniel 12:1,** "*And at that time shall Michael stand up, the great prince which standeth for the children of thy people: and there shall be a time of trouble, such as never was since there was a nation even to that same time: and at that time thy people shall be delivered, every one that shall be found written in the book.*"

It is referred to as "time of Jacob's trouble", and Christ called it "the great tribulation". He and Zechariah the prophet associate it with the return of the Lord.

Matthew 24:21-31, "²¹ *For then shall be great tribulation, such as was not since the beginning of the world to this time, no, nor ever shall be.*

²² And except those days should be shortened, there should no flesh be saved: but for the elect's sake those days shall be shortened.

²³ Then if any man shall say unto you, Lo, here is Christ, or there; believe it not.

²⁴ For there shall arise false Christs, and false prophets, and shall shew great signs and wonders; insomuch that, if it were possible, they shall deceive the very elect.

²⁵ Behold, I have told you before.

²⁶ Wherefore if they shall say unto you, Behold, he is in the desert; go not forth: behold, he is in the secret chambers; believe it not.

²⁷ For as the lightning cometh out of the east, and shineth even unto the west; so, shall also the coming of the Son of man be.

²⁸ For wheresoever the carcase is, there will the eagles be gathered together.

²⁹ Immediately after the tribulation of those days shall the sun be darkened, and the moon shall not give her light, and the stars shall fall from heaven, and the powers of the heavens shall be shaken:

³⁰ And then shall appear the sign of the Son of man in heaven: and then shall all the tribes of the earth mourn, and they shall see the Son of man coming in the clouds of heaven with power and great glory.

³¹ And he shall send his angels with a great sound of a trumpet, and they shall gather together his elect from the four winds, from one end of heaven to the other."

Zechariah 14:1-11, *"Behold, the day of the* LORD *cometh, and thy spoil shall be divided in the midst of thee.*

² For I will gather all nations against Jerusalem to battle; and the city shall be taken, and the houses rifled, and the women ravished; and half of the city shall go forth into captivity, and the residue of the people shall not be cut off from the city.

³ Then shall the LORD *go forth, and fight against those nations, as when he fought in the day of battle.*

⁴ And his feet shall stand in that day upon the mount of Olives, which is before Jerusalem on the east, and the mount of Olives shall cleave in the midst thereof toward the east and toward the west, and there shall be a very great valley; and half of the mountain shall remove toward the north, and half of it toward the south.

5 And ye shall flee to the valley of the mountains; for the valley of the mountains shall reach unto Azal: yea, ye shall flee, like as ye fled from before the earthquake in the days of Uzziah king of Judah: and the LORD my God shall come, and all the saints with thee.

6 And it shall come to pass in that day, that the light shall not be clear, nor dark:

7 But it shall be one day which shall be known to the LORD, not day, nor night: but it shall come to pass, that at evening time it shall be light.

8 And it shall be in that day, that living waters shall go out from Jerusalem; half of them toward the former sea, and half of them toward the hinder sea: in summer and in winter shall it be.

9 And the LORD shall be king over all the earth: in that day shall there be one LORD, and his name one.

10 All the land shall be turned as a plain from Geba to Rimmon south of Jerusalem: and it shall be lifted up, and inhabited in her place, from Benjamin's gate unto the place of the first gate, unto the corner gate, and from the tower of Hananeel unto the king's wine-presses.

[11] And men shall dwell in it, and there shall be no more utter destruction; but Jerusalem shall be safely inhabited."

The result of these terrible judgments will be that the Jews will call in their misery upon the Lord:

"And I will pour upon the 'House of David' and upon the inhabitance of Jerusalem the spirit of grace and as supplications."

Then Christ will come back to Jerusalem.

1. **Zechariah 12:10,** "*[10] And I will pour upon the house of David, and upon the inhabitants of Jerusalem, the spirit of grace and of supplications: and they shall look upon me whom they have pierced, and they shall mourn for him, as one mourned for his only son, and shall be in*

bitterness for him, as one that is in bitterness for his firstborn."

2. **Revelation 1:7,** *"⁷Behold, he cometh with clouds; and every eye shall see him, and they also which pierced him: and all kindreds of the earth shall wail because of him. Even so, Amen."*

3. **Zechariah 14:4,** *"⁴And his feet shall stand in that day upon the mount of Olives, which is before Jerusalem on the east, and the mount of Olives shall cleave in the midst thereof toward the east and toward the west, and there shall be a very great valley; and half of the mountain shall remove toward the north, and half of it toward the south."*

<u>THE JEWISH NATION SHALL BE BORN CONVERTED IN A DAY</u>

Isaiah 66:8, *"⁸Who hath heard such a thing? who hath seen such things? Shall the earth be made to bring forth in one day? or shall a nation be born at* *once? for as soon as Zion travailed, she brought forth her children."*

As the children of Israel took with them of the "riches of the Egyptians" when they came out of Egypt, so when they return to their own land in Israel will they take with them the riches of the Gentiles.

1. **Exodus 12:35-36,** *"[35] And the children of Israel did according to the word of Moses; and they borrowed of the Egyptians jewels of silver, and jewels of gold, and raiment: [36] And the LORD gave the people favour in the sight of the Egyptians, so that they lent unto them such things as they required. And they spoiled the Egyptians."*

2. **Isaiah 60:9,** *"[9] Surely the isles shall wait for me, and the ships of Tarshish first, to bring thy sons from far, their silver and their gold with them, unto the name of the LORD thy God, and to the Holy One of Israel, because he hath glorified thee."*

3. **Isaiah 61:6,** *"[6] But ye shall be named the Priests of the LORD: men shall call you the*

Ministers of our God: ye shall eat the riches of the Gentiles, and in their glory shall ye boast yourselves."

When they return Israel to their own land, it will be to possess and occupy all that was promised to Abraham.

"THE GLORY GRANT"

This was given by the almighty to Abraham, extending from the "River of Egypt unto the Great River, the River Euphrates".

Genesis 15:18, *"¹⁸ In the same day the* L*ord* *made a covenant with Abram, saying, unto thy seed have I given this land, from the river of Egypt unto the great river, the river Euphrates".*

And according to **Ezekiel 48:1-29**, the government shall be reestablished, and the nation of the Earth will be blessed through Israel.

Zechariah 8:20-23, "²⁰ Thus saith the LORD of hosts; It shall yet come to pass, that there shall come people, and the inhabitants of many cities:

²¹ And the inhabitants of one city shall go to another, saying, let us go speedily to pray before the LORD, and to seek the LORD of hosts: I will go also.

²² Yea, many people and strong nations shall come to seek the LORD of hosts in Jerusalem, and to pray before the LORD.

²³ Thus saith the LORD of hosts; In those days it shall come to pass, that ten men shall take hold out of all languages of the nations, even shall take hold of the skirt of him that is a Jew, saying, we will go with you: for we have heard that God is with you."

Ezekiel 37:1-14, "The hand of the LORD was upon me, and carried me out in the spirit of the LORD, and set me down in the **midst of the valley which was full of bones,**

²And caused me to pass by them round about: and, behold, there were very many in the open valley; and, lo, they were very dry.

³And he said unto me, **Son of man, can these bones live***? And I answered, O Lord GOD, thou knowest.*

⁴Again he said unto me, **Prophesy upon these bones***, and say unto them, O ye dry bones, hear the word of the LORD.*

⁵Thus saith the Lord GOD unto these bones; Behold, I will cause breath to enter into you, and ye shall live:

⁶And I will lay sinews upon you, and will bring up flesh upon you, and cover you with skin, and put breath in you, and ye shall live; and ye shall know that I am the LORD.

⁷So I prophesied as I was commanded: and as I prophesied, there was a noise, and behold a shaking, and the bones came together, bone to his bone.

8 And when I beheld, lo, the sinews and the flesh came up upon them, and the skin covered them above: but there was no breath in them.

9 Then said he unto me, Prophesy unto the wind, prophesy, son of man, and say to the wind, thus saith the Lord GOD; Come from the four winds, O breath, and **breathe upon these slain, that they may live.**

10 So I prophesied as he commanded me, and the breath came into them, and they lived, and stood up upon their feet, an exceeding great army.

11 Then he said unto me, Son of man, **these bones are the whole house of Israel**: *behold, they say,* **our bones are dried, and our hope is lost**: *we are cut off for our parts.*

12 Therefore prophesy and say unto them, thus saith the Lord GOD; Behold, O my people, **I will open your graves, and cause you to come up out of your graves,** *and bring you into the land of Israel.*

¹³ And ye shall know that I am the Lord, when I have opened your graves, O my people, and brought you up out of your graves,

¹⁴ **And shall put my spirit in you, and ye shall live**, and I shall place you in your own land: then shall ye know that I the Lord have spoken it, and performed it, saith the Lord."

2. SPIRITUAL RESURRECTION

This refers to those who are spiritually dead in "trespasses and sins."

Ephesians 2:1-6, "And you hath he quickened, who were dead in trespasses and sins;

² Wherein in time past ye walked according to the course of this world, according to the prince of the power of the air, the spirit that now worketh in the children of disobedience:

³ Among whom also we all had our conversation in times past in the lusts of our flesh, fulfilling the desires

of the flesh and of the mind; and were by nature the children of wrath, even as others.

⁴But God, who is rich in mercy, for his great love wherewith he loved us,

⁵Even when we were dead in sins, hath quickened us together with Christ, (by grace ye are saved;)

⁶And hath raised us up together, and made us sit together in heavenly places in Christ Jesus".

Ephesians 5:14, *"¹⁴Wherefore he saith, awake thou that sleepest, and arise from the dead, and Christ shall give thee light."*

Romans 6:11, *"¹¹Likewise reckon ye also your-selves to be dead indeed unto sin, but alive unto God through Jesus Christ our Lord."*

Colossians 2:13, *"¹³And you, being dead in your sins and the uncircumcision of your flesh, hath he quickened together with him, having forgiven you all trespasses".*

Colossians 1:23 "*²³If ye continue in the faith grounded and settled, and be not moved away from the hope of the gospel, which ye have heard, and which was preached to every creature which is under heaven; whereof I Paul am made a minister*".

This is a "present resurrection" and is going on continually. Every time a soul is born again, there is a passing from "Death" unto "Life", a "spiritual resurrection.

John 5:24, "*²⁴Verily, verily, I say unto you, He that heareth my word, and believeth on him that sent me, hath everlasting life, and shall not come into condemnation; but is passed from death unto life."*

John 3:16, "*For God so loved the world, that he gave his only begotten Son, that whosoever believeth in him should not perish, but have everlasting life."*

3. A MATERIAL RESURRECTION—THE PHYSICAL BODY

This is the resurrection of the dead body. The spirit of man does not die, it goes back to God who gave it.

Ecclesiastes 12:7, *"⁷Then shall the dust return to the earth as it was: and the spirit shall return unto God who gave it. The body."*

All that goes into the grave is the body, and all that can come out of the grave is the body.

The Resurrection of the Body

Jesus clearly and distinctly taught a resurrection from the grave.

John 5:28,29, *"²⁸Marvel not at this: for the hour is coming, in the which all that are in the graves shall hear his voice,*

29 And shall come forth; they that have done good, unto the resurrection of life; and they that have done evil, unto the resurrection of damnation."

Here, Jesus teaches the resurrection of both the "righteous" and the "wicked". The apostle Paul gave the same thing.

Acts 24:15, *"15 And have hope toward God, which they themselves also allow, that there shall be a resurrection of the dead, both of the just and unjust."*

For as in Adam all die (physically), even so in Christ shall all be made alive (physically).

1 Corinthians 15:22, *"22 For as in Adam all die, even so in Christ shall all be made alive."*

Here, the Apostle means (physical) Death and (physical) resurrection. This is clear, for it is the body and not the spirit.

These scriptures clearly teach that there is to be a resurrection of "all the dead", and if we did not look any further, we would be led to believe that the righteous and the wicked are not only to rise at the same time, but when we turn to the book of revelation, we find that the righteous are to rise "before" the wicked. They are not to simply precede them, but there is a space of a 1000 years between the two resurrections.

Revelation 20:4-5, "⁴*And I saw thrones, and they sat upon them, and judgment was given unto them: and I saw the souls of them that were beheaded for the witness of Jesus, and for the word of God, and which had not worshipped the beast, neither his image, neither had received his mark upon their foreheads, or in their hands; and they lived and reigned with Christ a thousand years.*

⁵But the rest of the dead lived not again until the thousand years were finished. This is the first resurrection."

"And I saw thrones, and they sat upon them, and judgment was given unto them."

This refers to the Saints of the first resurrection, who were represented by the "four and twenty elders", who in **Revelation 4:4** *"are seen seated on thrones surrounding the throne of God."*

Revelation 20:4, *"⁴And I saw thrones, and they sat upon them, and judgment was given unto them: and I saw the souls of them that were beheaded for the witness of Jesus, and for the word of God, and which had not worshipped the beast, neither his image, neither had received his mark upon their foreheads, or in their hands; and they lived and reigned with Christ a thousand years."*

These are the "Tribulation Saints" whom John first saw in their martyred condition as souls. Then he saw them rise from the dead. They lived again, and they with the first resurrection Saints reigned with Christ a thousand years.

But the rest of the dead, the wicked, lived not again until the thousand years were finished.

Revelation 20:6, "⁶ *Blessed and holy is he that hath part in the first resurrection: on such the second death hath no power, but they shall be priests of God and of Christ, and shall reign with him a thousand years."*

The doom of the wicked

Revelation 20:14-15, ¹⁴ *And death and hell were cast into the lake of fire. This is the second death.*

¹⁵ *And whosoever was not found written in the book of life was cast into the lake of fire."*

The dead are to rise in different order:

1 Corinthians 15:22-24, "²² *For as in Adam all die, even so in Christ shall all be made alive.*

²³ *But every man in his own order: Christ the first fruits; afterward they that are Christ's at his coming.*

²⁴ *Then cometh the end, when he shall have deliv-ered up the kingdom to God, even the Father; when*

he shall have put down all rule and all authority and power."

There has already been an "out resurrection" from "among the dead" when Jesus expired on the cross.

Matthew 27:50-53, *"⁵⁰ Jesus, when he had cried again with a loud voice, yielded up the ghost.*

⁵¹ And, behold, the veil of the temple was rent in twain from the top to the bottom; and the earth did quake, and the rocks rent;

⁵² And the graves were opened; and many bodies of the saints which slept arose,

⁵³ And came out of the graves after his resurrection, and went into the holy city, and appeared unto many."

Luke 20:35-36, *"³⁵ But they which shall be accounted worthy to obtain that world, and the resurrection from the dead, neither marry, nor are given in marriage:*

36 Neither can they die any more: for they are equal unto the angels; and are the children of God, being the children of the resurrection."

Luke 14:14, "*14 And thou shalt be blessed; for they cannot recompense thee: for thou shalt be recompensed at the resurrection of the just."*

Hebrews 11:35, "*35 Women received their dead raised to life again: and others were tortured, not accepting deliverance; that they might obtain a better resurrection".*

Philippians 3:11, "*11 If by any means I might attain unto the resurrection of the dead."*

1 Thessalonians 4:15-17, "*15 For this we say unto you by the word of the Lord, that we which are alive and remain unto the coming of the Lord shall not prevent them which are asleep.*

16 For the Lord himself shall descend from heaven with a shout, with the voice of the archangel, and with the trump of God: and the dead in Christ shall rise first:

¹⁷ Then we which are alive and remain shall be caught up together with them in the clouds, to meet the Lord in the air: and so, shall we ever be with the Lord.

Christ is to come back to usher in the Millennium, then that event must "proceed" the Millennium and be an "out resurrection" from among the dead, for the rest of the dead live not again until the 1000 years are finished. But the resurrection of the righteous and the wicked is not only to be different as to "time", but as to character.

John 5:28-29, *"²⁸ Marvel not at this: for the hour is coming, in the which all that are in the graves shall hear his voice,*

²⁹ And shall come forth; they that have done good, unto the resurrection of life; and they that have done evil, unto the resurrection of damnation."

Revelation 20:12-15, "[12] *And I saw the dead, small and great, stand before God; and the books were opened: and another book was opened, which is the book of life: and the dead were judged out of those things which were written in the books, according to their works.*

[13] And the sea gave up the dead which were in it; and death and hell delivered up the dead which were in them: and they were judged every man according to their works.

[14] And death and hell were cast into the lake of fire. This is the second death.

[15] And whosoever was not found written in the book of life was cast into the lake of fire."

This tells us that those who are raised at the second resurrection, or the resurrection of damnation, must appear at the great white throne judgment.

And that their name shall not be found written in the "book of life" and they shall be cast into the lake of fire, which is the second death.

The Manner of the Resurrection of the Body

1 Corinthians 15:35-54, "*35 But some man will say, how are the dead raised up? and with what body do they come?*

36 Thou fool, that which thou sowest is not quickened, except it die:

37 And that which thou sowest, thou sowest not that body that shall be, but bare grain, it may chance of wheat, or of some other grain:

38 But God giveth it a body as it hath pleased him, and to every seed his own body.

39 All flesh is not the same flesh: but there is one kind of flesh of men, another flesh of beasts, another of fishes, and another of birds.

⁴⁰ There are also celestial bodies, and bodies terrestrial: but the glory of the celestial is one, and the glory of the terrestrial is another.

⁴¹ There is one glory of the sun, and another glory of the moon, and another glory of the stars: for one star differeth from another star in glory.

⁴² So also is the resurrection of the dead. It is sown in corruption; it is raised in incorruption:

⁴³ It is sown in dishonour; it is raised in glory: it is sown in weakness; it is raised in power:

⁴⁴ It is sown a natural body; it is raised a spiritual body. There is a natural body, and there is a spiritual body.

⁴⁵ And so it is written, The first man Adam was made a living soul; the last Adam was made a quickening spirit.

⁴⁶ Howbeit that was not first which is spiritual, but that which is natural; and afterward that which is spiritual.

⁴⁷ *The first man is of the earth, earthy; the second man is the Lord from heaven.*

⁴⁸ *As is the earthy, such are they also that are earthy: and as is the heavenly, such are they also that are heavenly.*

⁴⁹ *And as we have borne the image of the earthy, we shall also bear the image of the heavenly.*

⁵⁰ *Now this I say, brethren, that flesh and blood cannot inherit the kingdom of God; neither doth corruption inherit incorruption.*

⁵¹ *Behold, I shew you a mystery; We shall not all sleep, but we shall all be changed,*

⁵² *In a moment, in the twinkling of an eye, at the last trump: for the trumpet shall sound, and the dead shall be raised incorruptible, and we shall be changed.*

⁵³ *For this corruptible must put on incorruption, and this mortal must put on immortality.*

⁵⁴ So when this corruptible shall have put on incorruption, and this mortal shall have put on immortality, then shall be brought to pass the saying that is written, Death is swallowed up in victory."

The Resurrection of the Death

1 Corinthians 15:42-44, *"⁴² So also is the resurrection of the dead. It is sown in corruption; it is raised in incorruption:*

⁴³ It is sown in dishonour; it is raised in glory: it is sown in weakness; it is raised in power:

⁴⁴ It is sown a natural body; it is raised a spiritual body. There is a natural body, and there is a spiritual body."

Christ's resurrected body is a sample of what ours is to be—flesh and bone.

Luke 24:39-43, *"³⁹ Behold my hands and my feet, that it is I myself: handle me, and see; for a spirit hath not flesh and bones, as ye see me have.*

⁴⁰ And when he had thus spoken, he shewed them his hands and his feet.

⁴¹ And while they yet believed not for joy, and wondered, he said unto them, Have ye here any meat?

⁴² And they gave him a piece of a broiled fish, and of a honeycomb.

⁴³ And he took it, and did eat before them."

Ephesians 5:30, *"³⁰ For we are members of his body, of his flesh, and of his bones.*

1 Corinthians 12:27, *"²⁷ Now ye are the body of Christ, and members in particular."*

THE BODY OF JESUS AFTER HIS RESURRECTION

The resurrection body shall be life in kind. It will be different in character and possess different qualities.

The Bible declares that all flesh is not the same flesh, but there is one kind of flesh of man, another flesh of beasts, another of fishes, and another of birds.

1 Corinthians 15:39, "*39 All flesh is not the same flesh: but there is one kind of flesh of men, another flesh of beasts, another of fishes, and another of birds.*"

That is how the flesh of God's creatures adapted to their environment.

"Fish flesh cannot fly in the air, nor bird flesh swim in the sea."

So, there are bodies **"terrestrial"** and bodies "**celestial**". One is a heavenly body and the other an earthly body.

1 Corinthians 15:40, *"⁴⁰ There are also celestial bodies, and bodies terrestrial: but the glory of the celestial is one, and the glory of the terrestrial is another."*

Celestial means:

1. A position in or relating to the sky, or outer space as observed in astronomy: a celestial body.

2. Belonging or relating to heaven. The Celestial city, Heaven divinity.

3. A heavenly or mythical being.

4. The word Celestial is primarily used to describe things that have to do with heavens, such as angels, spirits, stars and planets.

Terrestrial means of, on, or relating to the Earth. Terrestrial body.

The human body as it is now constituted could not exist in heaven. There must be a change, and this change is brought about by the resurrection.

1 Corinthians 15:42-44, *"⁴² So also is the resurrection of the dead. It is sown in corruption; it is raised in incorruption:*

⁴³ It is sown in dishonour; it is raised in glory: it is sown in weakness; it is raised in power:

⁴⁴ It is sown a natural body; it is raised a spiritual body. There is a natural body, and there is a spiritual body."

This does not mean that it will have no "substance".

Jesus Christ's resurrected body is a sample of what ours is to be.

While it is true that his body, Jesus' body, did not see corruption, and that He rose in the "same body" that was laid in the grave, and while it was the same in identity, "it was different in character". While the "nail prints" and spear wound were visible, it could pass through closed doors and appear and disappear at will. Yet, it still had "flesh and bone".

Luke 24:30-33, "*30 And it came to pass, as he sat at meat with them, he took bread, and blessed it, and brake, and gave to them.*

31 And their eyes were opened, and they knew him; and he vanished out of their sight.

32 And they said one to another, did not our heart burn within us, while he talked with us by the way, and while he opened to us the scriptures?

33 And they rose up the same hour, and returned to Jerusalem, and found the eleven gathered to-gether, and them that were with them".

But it did not have "blood", for "flesh and blood" cannot enter the Kingdom of God:

1 Corinthians 15:50, "*50 Now this I say, brethren, that flesh and blood cannot inherit the kingdom of God; neither doth corruption inherit incorruption."*

For blood is that which causes corruption.

To preserve a body, it must be drained of blood, or the blood chemically preserved by an embalming fluid. As the sacrifice was to be bled, so Jesus left his blood on the Earth.

As our resurrection bodies will have visible "form and shape", it stands to reason that they will have a framework of "**flesh and bone**". But it will be flesh and bone adapted to its new environment.

Ephesians 5:30, "*30 For we are members **of his body, of his flesh, and of his bones**.*"

We will have a Celestial body

2 Corinthians 12:2, "*2 I knew a man in Christ above fourteen years ago, (whether in the body, I cannot tell; or whether out of the body, I cannot tell: God knoweth;) such an one caught up to the third heaven.*"

2 Corinthians 12:4 "*4 How that he was caught up into paradise, and heard unspeakable words, which it is not lawful for a man to utter.*"

JESUS, THE LAST ADAM

The scriptures speak of two representative men, and the first is called Adam. The second is called the last Adam, or the second man the Lord from Heaven.

1 Corinthians 15:45, "*⁵And so it is written, the first man Adam was made a living soul; the last Adam was made a quickening spirit.*"

This identifies Him with the Lord Jesus Christ. The first Adam is charged with bringing sin into the world. "By one-man sin entered into the world, and death by sin; and so, death passed upon all men, for that all have sinned".

Romans 5:12, "*¹²Wherefore, as by one-man sin entered into the world, and death by sin; and so, death passed upon all men, for that all have sinned*".

The last Adam came to reverse what the first Adam did. And to put away sin.

Hebrews 9:26, "*26 For then must he often have suffered since the foundation of the world: but now once in the end of the world hath he appeared to put away sin by the sacrifice of himself.*"

Romans 5:17, "*17 For if by one man's offence death reigned by one; much more they which receive abundance of grace and of the gift of righteousness shall reign in life by one, Jesus Christ.*"

To understand the work of these two representative men, we must study their history.

THE FIRST ADAM

After the Earth had been restored from its "formless and void" condition, and the air, sea, and Earth been repopulated with fish and animal life, we read:

Genesis 1:26-27, "*26 And God said, let us make man in our image, after our likeness: and let them have dominion over the fish of the sea, and over the fowl of the air, and over the cattle, and over all the* *earth, and over every creeping thing that creepeth upon the earth.*

²⁷ So God created man in his own image, in the image of God created he him; male and female created he them."

From this we see that man is a created being, that he was made in the "image of God", not in the Image of an "Ape", and was formed not from a brute, but of the dust of the Earth.

The whole human race is of its "own species" and had a common origin.

Acts 17:26, "*²⁶ And hath made of one blood all nations of men for to dwell on all the face of the earth, and hath determined the times before appointed, and the bounds of their habitation*".

We are told that "The Lord God formed (fashioned) man of the dust of the ground, and breath into his nostrils the breath of life; and man became a living soul". From this we see that the creation of man was threefold:

2. The formation of the body,

3. The impartation of the spirit, and

4. The unification of the two through the soulish part of Man.

The two principal parts of man are the body and the spirit, but the functions of these are separate: one being physical and the other spiritual.

A third part had to be supplied to be the intermediate between them, called the Soul, through which they may communicate.

This makes man a threefold being.

1 Thessalonians 5:23, *"23 And the very God of peace sanctify you wholly; and I pray God your whole spirit and soul and body be preserved blameless unto the coming of our Lord Jesus Christ."*

Hebrews 4:12, *"12 For the word of God is quick, and powerful, and sharper than any two-edged sword,* *piercing even to the dividing asunder of soul and spirit, and of the joints and marrow, and is a discerner of the thoughts and intents of the heart."*

In Adam as originally created, the "Soul" was such a perfect medium of communication between the body and the spirit that there was no conflict between them. The three blended together in one harmonious whole.

When man fell, or sinned, the "Soul" became the "battlefield" of the body and the spirit and the conflict began.

Romans 7:7-24 gives us a graphic picture.

Romans 7:7-24, *"⁷ What shall we say then? Is the law sin? God forbids. Nay, I had not known sin, but by the law: for I had not known lust, except the law had said, thou shalt not covet.*

⁸ But sin, taking occasion by the commandment, wrought in me all manner of concupiscence. For without the law sin was dead.

⁹ For I was alive without the law once: but when the commandment came, sin revived, and I died.

¹⁰ And the commandment, which was ordained to life, I found to be unto death.

¹¹ For sin, taking occasion by the commandment, deceived me, and by it slew me.

¹² Wherefore the law is holy, and the commandment holy, and just, and good.

¹³ Was then that which is good made death unto me? God forbids. But sin, that it might appear sin, working death in me by that which is good; that sin by the commandment might become exceeding sinful.

¹⁴ For we know that the law is spiritual: but I am carnal, sold under sin.

¹⁵ For that which I do I allow not: for what I would, that do I not; but what I hate, that do I.

¹⁶ If then I do that which I would not, I consent unto the law that it is good.

¹⁷ Now then it is no more I that do it, but sin that dwelleth in me.

¹⁸ For I know that in me (that is, in my flesh,) dwelleth no good thing: for to will is present with me; but how to perform that which is good I find not.

¹⁹ For the good that I would I do not: but the evil which I would not, that I do.

²⁰ Now if I do that I would not, it is no more I that do it, but sin that dwelleth in me.

²¹ I find then a law, that, when I would do good, evil is present with me.

²² For I delight in the law of God after the inward man:

²³ But I see another law in my members, warring against the law of my mind, and bringing me into captivity to the law of sin which is in my members.

²⁴ O wretched man that I am! who shall deliver me from the body of this death?"

Galatians 5:16-21, "[16] *This I say then, walk in the Spirit, and ye shall not fulfil the lust of the flesh.*

[17] For the flesh lusteth against the Spirit, and the Spirit against the flesh: and these are contrary the one to the other: so that ye cannot do the things that ye would.

[18] But if ye be led of the Spirit, ye are not under the law.

[19] Now the works of the flesh are manifest, which are these; Adultery, fornication, uncleanness, lasciviousness,

[20] Idolatry, witchcraft, hatred, variance, emulations, wrath, strife, seditions, heresies,

[21] Envyings, murders, drunkenness, revellings, and such like: of the which I tell you before, as I have also told you in time past, that they which do such things shall not inherit the kingdom of God."

Romans 3:20, *"²⁰ Therefore by the deeds of the law there shall no flesh be justified in his sight: for by the law is the knowledge of sin."*

Eve was not fashioned in the same way as Adam; she was made later.

Genesis 2:21-23, *"²¹ And the L*ORD *God caused a deep sleep to fall upon Adam, and he slept: and he took one of his ribs, and closed up the flesh instead thereof;*

*²² And the rib, which the L*ORD *God had taken from man, made he a woman, and brought her unto the man.*

²³ And Adam said, this is now bone of my bones, and flesh of my flesh: she shall be called Woman, because she was taken out of Man."

The reason why Eve was not fashioned separately from Adam, but was taken out of Adam's side, was to show that in their relation to each other as man and wife they were to be one flesh.

That is in their interest's sympathies. They were to be one, and physically they were to be counterparts of each other. In this respect, Adam and Eve are a type of the last Adam and his Eve—the Church.

Ephesians 5:25-32, "*25 Husbands, love your wives, even as Christ also loved the church, and gave himself for it;*

26 That he might sanctify and cleanse it with the washing of water by the word,

27 That he might present it to himself a glorious church, not having spot, or wrinkle, or any such thing; but that it should be holy and without blemish.

28 So ought men to love their wives as their own bodies. He that loveth his wife loveth himself.

29 For no man ever yet hated his own flesh; but nourisheth and cherisheth it, even as the Lord the church:

30 For we are members of his body, of his flesh, and of his bones.

³¹ For this cause shall a man leave his father and mother, and shall be joined unto his wife, and they two shall be one flesh.

³² This is a great mystery: but I speak concerning Christ and the church."

Adam was created as a full-grown man, perfect in intellect and knowledge. Adam named the Beasts of the field and the fowls of the air.

Genesis 2:19, *"¹⁹ And out of the ground the LORD God formed every beast of the field, and every fowl of the air; and brought them unto Adam to see what he would call them: and whatsoever Adam called every living creature, that was the name thereof."*

Why God did not forewarn Adam of the danger of an attack by Satan, let it not be forgotten that the commandment not to eat of the "Tree of knowledge of good and evil" should have caused him to beware of any being who should tempt him to disobey the command of God and eat of it?

To have plainly told him Adam of the plan of Satan would have frustrated God's purpose in the testing of Adam. True obedience is to obey without knowing why.

Adam and Eve were created "innocent". Innocence is not "righteousness". Innocence cannot become righteousness until tested. If Adam and Eve had withstood the "test", they would have become "righteous" or "Holy". They failed, and instead became sinners. There is but one step from innocence to holiness, or from innocence to sin.

Adam and Eve took the step from innocence to sin and became sinners. If they had taken the opposite step, they would have become "Holy" and been beyond the possibility of "sin". No man can become "Holy" without the new birth.

The first effect of the disobedience of Adam and Eve was "self-consciousness" when they saw that they were naked.

Genesis 3:7,8-10, "⁷*And the eyes of them both were opened, and they knew that they were naked; and they sewed fig leaves together, and made themselves aprons.*

⁸*And they heard the voice of the LORD God walking in the garden in the cool of the day: and Adam and his wife hid themselves from the presence of the LORD God amongst the trees of the garden.*

⁹*And the LORD God called unto Adam, and said unto him, Where art thou?*

¹⁰*And he said, I heard thy voice in the garden, and I was afraid, because I was naked; and I hid myself.*"

Adam and Eve at first wore no clothing, nor did they need to. Their state of innocence made them not ashamed.

Clothing may hide our shame form the eyes of man, but not from the eyes of God.

Hebrews 4:13, "¹³*Neither is there any creature that is not manifest in his sight: but all things are* *naked and opened unto the eyes of him with whom we have to do."*

Ezekiel 11:5, *"⁵ And the Spirit of the LORD fell upon me, and said unto me, speak; Thus, saith the LORD; Thus, have ye said, O house of Israel: for I know the things that come into your mind, every one of them."*

Isaiah 46:10, *"¹⁰ Declaring the end from the beginning, and from ancient times the things that are not yet done, saying, my counsel shall stand, and I will do all my pleasure".*

Job 34:21, *"²¹ For his eyes is upon the ways of man, and he seeth all his goings."*

God came down to take his usual walk in the Garden in the cool of the day.

Genesis 3:8, *"⁸ And they heard the voice of the LORD God walking in the garden in the cool of the day: and Adam and his wife hid themselves from the* *presence of the LORD God amongst the trees of the garden."*

Heretofore, they had looked forward to the daily visit of the Lord God, but now they feared to face him. Thus, sin makes cowards of us all.

Genesis 3:10, *"¹⁰ And he said, I heard thy voice in the garden, and I was afraid, because I was naked; and I hid myself."*

When questioning them, the Lord God got them to sit in judgment on their own conduct. Adam blamed his fall on Eve; she blamed her fall on the serpent. God patiently listened to them and gave them an opportunity to justify their conduct, then He passed judgment on them. But to the serpent, he gave no opportunity for justification, but said:

Genesis 3:14, *"¹⁴ And the LORD God said unto the serpent, because thou hast done this, thou art cursed above all cattle, and above every beast of the field; upon thy belly shalt thou go, and dust shalt thou eat all the days of thy life".*

Thy seed and her seed, it (her seed)—Christ shall bruise thy head, and thou shalt bruise his heel.

In the expression "thy seed" (Satan's seed) we have a prophetic reference to the Antichrist, who as Satan's seed is called in **2 Thessalonians 2:3,** the "son of perdition".

2 Thessalonians 2:3, "*³ Let no man deceive you by any means: for that day shall not come, except there comes a falling away first, and that man of sin be revealed, the son of perdition".*

These are the word of a judge to his condemned criminal, who is awaiting sentence, and is a confirmation of Satan's previous rebellion.

John 16:11, "*¹¹ Of judgment, because the prince of this world is judged."*

John 12:31, "*³¹ Now is the judgment of this world: now shall the prince of this world be cast out."*

Romans 16:20, "²⁰ And the God of peace shall bruise Satan under your feet shortly. The grace of our Lord Jesus Christ be with you. Amen."

Revelation 12:7-8,10-11, "⁷ And there was war in heaven: Michael and his angels fought against the dragon; and the dragon fought and his angels,

⁸ And prevailed not; neither was their place found any more in heaven."

Revelation 12:10-11, "¹⁰ And I heard a loud voice saying in heaven, Now is come salvation, and strength, and the kingdom of our God, and the power of his Christ: for the accuser of our brethren is cast down, which accused them before our God day and night.

¹¹ And they overcame him by the blood of the Lamb, and by the word of their testimony; and they loved not their lives unto the death.

Revelation 20:10, "¹⁰ And the devil that deceived them was cast into the lake of fire and brimstone,

where the beast and the false prophet are, and shall
be tormented day and night for ever and ever."

THE LAST ADAM: JESUS

The fall of the "First Adam" demanded the coming of the "last Adam".

It is self-evident that a fallen creature cannot redeem itself. It must be redeemed by a power outside itself.

Therefore, no human being of the Adamic race could redeem the race; such a redemption demanded a divine interposition, but the redeemer must have the same nature as the Adamic race.

He must be a man, and to this end he must be born into the human race and yet be free from the "taint of sin".

This was accomplished by the "Virgin Birth".

Having taken upon himself human nature, it was necessary that the last Adam, Jesus, be put to the same test as the "first Adam".

To this end, we read that immediately after his Baptism, Jesus, before He had preached a sermon or called a disciple, was led of the Holy spirit into the "wilderness" to be tempted (tested) of the devil.

Matthew 4:1-11, *"Then was Jesus led up of the Spirit into the wilderness to be tempted of the devil.*

²And when he had fasted forty days and forty nights, he was afterward an hungred.

³And when the tempter came to him, he said, If thou be the Son of God, command that these stones be made bread.

⁴But he answered and said, it is written, Man shall not live by bread alone, but by every word that pro-ceedeth out of the mouth of God.

⁵Then the devil taketh him up into the holy city, and setteth him on a pinnacle of the temple,

⁶And saith unto him, if thou be the Son of God, cast thyself down: for it is written, He shall give his angels charge concerning thee: and in their hands they shall bear thee up, lest at any time thou dash thy foot against a stone.

⁷Jesus said unto him, it is written again, thou shalt not tempt the Lord thy God.

⁸Again, the devil taketh him up into an exceeding high mountain, and sheweth him all the kingdoms of the world, and the glory of them;

⁹And saith unto him, all these things will I give thee, if thou wilt fall down and worship me.

¹⁰Then saith Jesus unto him, get thee hence, Satan: for it is written, thou shalt worship the Lord thy God, and him only shalt thou serve.

¹¹Then the devil leaveth him, and, behold, angels came and ministered unto him."

It was not then a case of it just "happening so"; it was a part of God's plan as to the "last Adam, Jesus".

The temptation was not planned by the devil. He doubtless would have avoided it, for He knew who Jesus was, but Jesus had been led into the rendezvous.

(Rendezvous means a meeting at an agreed time and place, typically between two people.)

The purpose of Jesus' temptation was to show that He was qualified to be the head of a new race. The timing of the temptation of his sonship and the proclamation of the Kingdom is not without significance, for it explains the character of the temptations as having a bearing on the setting up and feeding the subjects of the Kingdom.

Could Jesus have sinned? NO

Jesus was the only begotten son of God, born of the "Virgin Mary", and it was said of the body of Jesus that it was "that Holy thing": Therefore, the humanity of Jesus was sinless, and when joined to the eternally holy personality of the son, there could have been no possibility of Jesus sinning.

1 John 3:9, "*9 Whosoever is born of God doth not commit sin; for his seed remaineth in him: and he cannot sin, because he is born of God.*"

1 John 5:18, "*18 We know that whosoever is born of God sinneth not; but he that is begotten of God keepeth himself, and that wicked one toucheth him not.*"

Jesus was the lamb foreordained before the foundation of the world.

1 Peter 1:18-20, "*18 Forasmuch as ye know that ye were not redeemed with corruptible things, as silver and gold, from your vain conversation received by tradition from your fathers;*

19 But with the precious blood of Christ, as of a lamb without blemish and without spot:

20 Who verily was foreordained before the foundation of the world, but was manifest in these last times for you".

A lamb accepted for sacrifice must be "without spot or blemish", The scriptures thus declare that whosoever is born of God cannot sin.

1 John 3:9, *"⁹ Whosoever is born of God doth not commit sin; for his seed remaineth in him: and he cannot sin, because he is born of God."*

Jesus, therefore, could not sin. If He could have sinned at the temptation, since there had been no change in his nature since then—for he took his nature his humanity back with him to heaven—what is there no prevent him yielding to temptation in the future?

What guarantee have we that the whole plan of salvation shall not yet be upset? The thought is contrary to the whole trend of the scripture.

What, then, was the purpose of the temptation if it were not possible for Jesus to have fallen?

The purpose was simply to show that Jesus was a perfect savior, and that there was no sin in him nor possibility of failure.

He was thus set before us not as an example to be followed when we are tempted, but as an object of faith to whom to look as our deliverer when we are tempted.

So, the temptation of Jesus was the test of his sonship and of his power to overcome and destroy the work of the devil, and to show that we need no longer fear, but that he is a perfect and all-powerful savior.

As we have seen, the first Adam brought upon the human race guilt, condemnation, and separation, so the last Adam, Jesus, reverses all these and the standing of the believer is that of "no guilt".

"No longer under condemnation", and for him there shall be "No separation" from God.

Romans 8:33-34,38-39, "33 *Who shall lay anything to the charge of God's elect? It is God that justifieth.*

34 Who is he that condemneth? It is Christ that died, yea rather, that is risen again, who is even at the right hand of God, who also maketh intercession for us.

38 For I am persuaded, that neither death, nor life, nor angels, nor principalities, nor powers, nor things present, nor things to come,

39 Nor height, nor depth, nor any other creature, shall be able to separate us from the love of God, which is in Christ Jesus our Lord."

The wages of sin are death, but the bible said in **1 Corinthians 15:22**, *"22 For as in Adam all die, even so in Christ shall all be made alive."*

And He is speaking only to the body and not of the soul, so the universalist cannot find an argument here for universal salvation, "as in Adam all die (physically), so in Christ shall all be made alive (physically)".

So, as the first Adam brough death into the world, the last Adam, Jesus, brought "resurrection, life, and "immortality" to light through the Gospel.

The spirit of the life

Romans 8:10, "*[10] And if Christ be in you, the body is dead because of sin; but the Spirit is life because of righteousness.*"

John 6:63, "*[63] It is the spirit that quickeneth; the flesh profiteth nothing: the words that I speak unto you, they are spirit, and they are life.*"

Genesis 2:7, "*[7] And the LORD God formed man of the dust of the ground, and breathed into his nostrils the breath of life; and man became a living soul.*"

Job 27:3, "*[3] All the while my breath is in me, and the spirit of God is in my nostrils*".

Job 32:8, "*[8] But there is a spirit in man: and the inspiration of the Almighty giveth them understanding.*"

Ezekiel 37:1-14, "*The hand of the LORD was upon me, and carried me out in the spirit of the LORD, and set me down in the midst of the valley which was full of bones,*

²And caused me to pass by them round about: and, behold, there were very many in the open valley; and, lo, they were very dry.

³And he said unto me, Son of man, can these bones live? And I answered, O Lord GOD, thou knowest.

⁴Again he said unto me, Prophesy upon these bones, and say unto them, O ye dry bones, hear the word of the LORD.

⁵Thus saith the Lord GOD unto these bones; Behold, I will cause breath to enter into you, and ye shall live:

⁶And I will lay sinews upon you, and will bring up flesh upon you, and cover you with skin, and put breath in you, and ye shall live; and ye shall know that I am the LORD.

⁷So I prophesied as I was commanded: and as I prophesied, there was a noise, and behold a shaking, and the bones came together, bone to his bone.

8And when I beheld, lo, the sinews and the flesh came up upon them, and the skin covered them above: but there was no breath in them.

9Then said he unto me, Prophesy unto the wind, prophesy, son of man, and say to the wind, thus saith the Lord GOD; Come from the four winds, O breath, and breathe upon these slain, that they may live.

10So I prophesied as he commanded me, and the breath came into them, and they lived, and stood up upon their feet, an exceeding great army.

11Then he said unto me, Son of man, these bones are the whole house of Israel: behold, they say, our bones are dried, and our hope is lost: we are cut off for our parts.

12Therefore prophesy and say unto them, thus saith the Lord GOD; Behold, O my people, I will open your graves, and cause you to come up out of your graves, and bring you into the land of Israel.

*13And ye shall know that I am the L*O*RD, when I have opened your graves, O my people, and brought you up out of your graves,*

*14And shall put my spirit in you, and ye shall live, and I shall place you in your own land: then shall ye know that I the L*O*RD have spoken it, and performed it, saith the L*O*RD."*

THE RESURRECTION OF THE SAINT'S BODY—THE BELIEVER

Romans 6:3-10, "*³Know ye not, that so many of us as were baptized into Jesus Christ were baptized into his death?*

⁴Therefore we are buried with him by baptism into death: that like as Christ was raised up from the dead by the glory of the Father, even so we also should walk in newness of life.

⁵For if we have been planted together in the likeness of his death, we shall be also in the likeness of his resurrection:

⁶Knowing this, that our old man is crucified with him, that the body of sin might be destroyed, that henceforth we should not serve sin.

⁷For he that is dead is freed from sin.

⁸Now if we be dead with Christ, we believe that we shall also live with him:

⁹Knowing that Christ being raised from the dead dieth no more; death hath no more dominion over him.

¹⁰For in that he died, he died unto sin once: but in that he liveth, he liveth unto God."

The scriptures are full of the "supernatural". The only cure for the "materialism" of the present day is to discover what the scriptures reveal as to the "spirit-world".

There is but a step from the "natural world" to the "spirit world". The dividing veil is our "fleshy" bodies.

The "heavenlies" are people with spirit beings.

MAN'S REVELATION TO THE "SPIRIT WORLD"

Man, in his physical and spiritual makeup, was made for two worlds: the physical and the spiritual world.

1 Thessalonians 5:23, "*²³And the very God of peace sanctify you wholly; and I pray God your whole spirit and soul and body be preserved blameless unto the coming of our Lord Jesus Christ.*"

"I pray God your whole 'Spirit' and 'Soul' and 'Body' be preserved blameless unto the coming of our Lord Jesus Christ."

Hebrews 4:12, "*¹²For the word of God is quick, and powerful, and sharper than any two-edged sword, piercing even to the dividing asunder of soul and spirit, and of the joints and marrow, and is a discerner of the thoughts and intents of the heart.*"

From these scriptures, we see that man is a trinity, and is composed of body, soul, and spirit. Man was made in the image of God, and God is a trinity.

When a man dies, his soul and spirit separate from the body and the body is laid in the grave. But the spirit is not bodiless; it has a physical, or soulish body.

The soulish body can hear and speak and think and feel, so it must have some tangible form.

It is not a ghostlike structure; there is no limitation in its use, or there would be no need for it to recover its physical body at the resurrection.

There is such a thing as the soulish body. It is described in **Luke 16:19-31,** the rich and Lazarus:

Luke 16:19-31, "*[19] There was a certain rich man, which was clothed in purple and fine linen, and fared sumptuously every day:*

[20] And there was a certain beggar named Lazarus, which was laid at his gate, full of sores,

[21] And desiring to be fed with the crumbs which fell from the rich man's table: moreover, the dogs came and licked his sores.

22 And it came to pass, that the beggar died, and was carried by the angels into Abraham's bosom: the rich man also died, and was buried;

23 And in hell he lifts up his eyes, being in torments, and seeth Abraham afar off, and Lazarus in his bosom.

24 And he cried and said, Father Abraham, have mercy on me, and send Lazarus, that he may dip the tip of his finger in water, and cool my tongue; for I am tormented in this flame.

25 But Abraham said, Son, remember that thou in thy lifetime receivedst thy good things, and likewise Lazarus evil things: but now he is comforted, and thou art tormented.

26 And beside all this, between us and you there is a great gulf fixed: so that they which would pass from hence to you cannot; neither can they pass to us, that would come from thence.

27 Then he said, I pray thee therefore, father, that thou wouldest send him to my father's house:

²⁸For I have five brethren; that he may testify unto them, lest they also come into this place of torment.

²⁹Abraham saith unto him, they have Moses and the prophets; let them hear them.

³⁰And he said, Nay, father Abraham: but if one went unto them from the dead, they will repent.

³¹And he said unto him, if they hear not Moses and the prophets, neither will they be persuaded, though one rose from the dead."

The story is not a parable, but a description by Jesus Christ of something that really happens when you die.

Jesus declares that both Lazarus and the rich man died and were buried. That is, their bodies were left on the earth.

But what happened to them or the Saint body in the underworld? Jesus give a descriptive of what happened to them the Saint body, in their disembodied state.

In that state, they were conscious, and the rich man recognized Lazarus, which he could not have done if Lazarus had not had a body—not his physical body he left that on the Earth, but his soulish body.

This is proof that the soulish body is not simply a body, but one whose outward form and appearance conforms to the earthly body of the owner; otherwise he would not be recognizable in the other world.

Again, the rich man could see and feel and thirst, and talk, and remember, proving that he possessed his sense and had not lost his personality.

This also proves that there is no break, or "soul sleep", in the continuity of existence, or consciousness, in passing from the "earth life to the spirit life".

Sleep in the scripture always refers to the body, not to the soul, and the expression "asleep in Jesus" refers to the believer only.

John 11:11, *"[11] These things said he: and after that he saith unto them, our friend Lazarus sleepeth; but I go, that I may awake him out of sleep."*

Let us trace the life of the soul and spirit after they have left the body. In the account of the rich man and Lazarus we have a description of the underworld.

The underworld is made up of two compartments, paradise and hell (not the final hell—that is Gehenna, the lake of fire) with an impassable gulf between.

Now, before the resurrection of Christ Jesus, our Lord and savior, the soul and spirit of the righteous dead went to the paradise compartment of the underworld. There, Jesus Christ met the thief after his death on the cross.

On the day of his resurrection, Jesus Christ's soul and spirit returned from the underworld. But he did not return alone. He brough back with him all the occupants of the paradise compartment and locked it up, and he now has the keys of death and hell, or Hades.

In Revelation 1:18, he has the keys:

Revelation 1:18, "*18 I am he that liveth, and was dead; and, behold, I am alive for evermore, amen; and have the keys of hell and of death."*

Ephesians 4:8-10, he is brought back from the underworld:

Ephesians 4:8-10, "*8 Wherefore he saith, when he ascended up on high, he led captivity captive, and gave gifts unto men.*

9 (Now that he ascended, what is it but that he also descended first into the lower parts of the earth?

10 He that descended is the same also that ascended up far above all heavens, that he might fill all things.)"

Those that died in faith:

In **Hebrews 11:13**, those who came back from the underworld with Jesus Christ got their bodies and ascended with him as the "first fruits of the resurrection from among the dead".

Hebrews 11:13, "*13 These all died in faith, not having received the promises, but having seen them afar off, and were persuaded of them, and embraced them, and confessed that they were strangers and pilgrims on the earth.*"

Matthew 27:50-53, "*50 Jesus, when he had cried again with a loud voice, yielded up the ghost.*

51 And, behold, the veil of the temple was rent in twain from the top to the bottom; and the earth did quake, and the rocks rent;

52 And the graves were opened; and many bodies of the saints which slept arose,

53 And came out of the graves after his resurrection, and went into the holy city, and appeared unto many."

The rest were taken up to the "third Heaven", where Paul was caught up:

In **2 Corinthians 12:1-4,** Paul called it "paradise, there all the righteous dead" that have died since Jesus Christ's resurrection go that they may be "with the Lord".

2 Corinthians 12:1-4, *"It is not expedient for me doubtless to glory. I will come to visions and revelations of the Lord.*

2I knew a man in Christ above fourteen years ago, (whether in the body, I cannot tell; or whether out of the body, I cannot tell: God knoweth;) such an one caught up to the third heaven.

3And I knew such a man, (whether in the body, or out of the body, I cannot tell: God knoweth;)

4How that he was caught up into paradise, and heard unspeakable words, which it is not lawful for a man to utter."

Philippians 1:23, *"23For I am in a strait betwixt two, having a desire to depart, and to be with Christ; which is far better".*

2 Corinthians 5:8, "*8 We are confident, I say, and willing rather to be absent from the body, and to be present with the Lord.*"

There, the "souls of the righteous dead" shall remain until the time come for the resurrection of their bodies. Then when Jesus Christ comes back to meet his Church in the Air, He will bring back the souls of the "righteous dead" from the paradise of the third heaven, for we are told that he will bring them whose bodies "Sleep in Christ Jesus" on the Earth with him.

In **1 Thessalonians 4:14,** they will continue on to the Earth and get their "bodies" from the grave, and then ascend again together with the "translated Saints" to meet the Lord in the air.

1 Thessalonians 4:14, "*14 For if we believe that Jesus died and rose again, even so them also which sleep in Jesus will God bring with him.*"

Now the "wicked dead" are still in the Hell compartment of the underworld, and will remain there until the second resurrection.

Revelation 20:5-6, "*⁵But the rest of the dead lived not again until the thousand years were finished. This is the first resurrection.*

⁶Blessed and holy is he that hath part in the first resurrection: on such the second death hath no power, but they shall be priests of God and of Christ, and shall reign with him a thousand years."

When the wicked dead return to the earth from hell and get their bodies, they then go to the "Great white Throne" judgment. After judgment, they will be sentenced to the "second death", which means that they shall die again in the sense of losing their bodies the second time. And as "disembodied spirit", they will be cast in to the "lake of fire" (Gehenna, the final Hell).

There, they will suffer in flames forever. As soul and spirit are impervious to flames, this explains how the wicked, after being disembodied again by the second death, can exist forever in literal fire.

Mark 9:43-48, "*43 And if thy hand offends thee, cut it off: it is better for thee to enter into life maimed, than having two hands to go into hell, into the fire that never shall be quenched:*

44 Where their worm dieth not, and the fire is not quenched.

45 And if thy foot offends thee, cut it off: it is better for thee to enter halt into life, than having two feet to be cast into hell, into the fire that never shall be quenched:

46 Where their worm dieth not, and the fire is not quenched.

47 And if thine eye offend thee, pluck it out: it is better for thee to enter into the kingdom of God with one eye, than having two eyes to be cast into hell fire:

48 Where their worm dieth not, and the fire is not quenched."

THE THREEFOLD NATURE OF MAN

Body, Soul and Spirit

1 Thessalonians 5:23, "*²³And the very God of peace sanctify you wholly; and I pray God your whole spirit and soul and body be preserved blameless unto the coming of our Lord Jesus Christ.*"

BODY: **Galatians 5:16-17,** "*¹⁶This I say then, walk in the Spirit, and ye shall not fulfil the lust of the flesh.*

¹⁷For the flesh lusteth against the Spirit, and the Spirit against the flesh: and these are contrary the one to the other: so that ye cannot do the things that ye would."

THE BODY HAS FIVE COMPONENTS

1. Sight

2 Corinthians 5:7, "*⁷For we walk by faith, not by* **sight**".

Genesis 2:9, "*⁹And out of the ground made the LORD God to grow every tree that is pleasant to the **sight**, and good for food; the tree of life also in the midst of the garden, and the tree of knowledge of good and evil.*"

Genesis 19:19, "*¹⁹Indeed now, your servant has found favor in your **sight**, and you have increased your mercy which you have shown me by saving my life; but I cannot escape to the mountains, lest some evil overtake me and I die.*"

Exodus 3:3, "*³Then Moses said, "I will now turn aside and see this great **sight**, why the bush does not burn.*"

2. Smell

Philippians 4:18, "*¹⁸But I have all, and abound: I am full, having received of Epaphroditus the things which were sent from you, an odour of a **sweet smell**, a sacrifice acceptable, well pleasing to God.*"

Isaiah 3:24, "*24 And it shall come to pass, that instead of sweet **smell** there shall be stink; and instead of a girdle a rent; and instead of well-set hair baldness; and instead of a stomacher a girding of sackcloth; and burning instead of beauty.*"

Leviticus 26:31, "*31 And I will make your cities waste, and bring your sanctuaries unto desolation, and I will not **smell** the savour of your sweet odours.*"

Song of Solomon 4:11, "*11 Thy lips, O my spouse, drop as the honeycomb: honey and milk are under thy tongue; and the **smell** of thy garments is like the **smell** of Lebanon.*"

3. Hearing

Romans 10:17, "*17 So then faith cometh by hearing, and hearing by the word of God.*"

Ecclesiastes 5:1, "*Keep thy foot when thou goest to the house of God, and be more ready to hear, than to give the sacrifice of fools: for they consider not that they do evil.*"

Mark 12:29 "*29 And Jesus answered him, the first of all the commandments is, Hear, O Israel; The Lord our God is one Lord".*

4. Taste

Psalm 34:8 "*8 O **taste** and see that the LORD is good: blessed is the man that trusteth in him.*"

Exodus 16:31, "*31 And the house of Israel called the name thereof Manna: and it was like coriander seed, white; and the **taste** of it was like wafers made with honey.*"

John 2:9, "*9 When the ruler of the feast had **tasted** the water that was made wine, and knew not whence it was: (but the servants which drew the water knew;) the governor of the feast called the bridegroom".*

Job 6:6 "*6 Can that which is unsavoury be eaten without salt? or is there any **taste** in the white of an egg?*"

Psalm 119:103, "*103 How sweet are thy words unto my **taste**! yea, sweeter than honey to my mouth!*"

5. Touch

Isaiah 52:11, "*11 Depart ye, depart ye, go ye out from thence, **touch** no unclean thing; go ye out of the midst of her; be ye clean, that bear the vessels of the LORD.*"

Jeremiah 1:9, "*9 Then the LORD put forth his hand, and **touched** my mouth. And the LORD said unto me, Behold, I have put my words in thy mouth.*"

Exodus 30:29, "*29 And thou shalt sanctify them, that they may be most holy: whatsoever **touch** them shall be holy.*"

Luke 5:13 "*13 And he put forth his hand, and **touched** him, saying, I will: be thou clean. And immediately the leprosy departed from him.*"

<u>SOUL</u>: Genesis 2:7, "*7 And the LORD God formed man of the dust of the ground, and breathed into his* *nostrils the breath of life; and man became a living soul."*

THE SOUL HAS FIVE COMPONENTS

1. Conscience:

1 Timothy 4:1-2 *"Now the Spirit speaketh expressly, that in the latter times some shall depart from the faith, giving heed to seducing spirits, and doctrines of devils; ²Speaking lies in hypocrisy; having their **conscience** seared with a hot iron".*

Titus 1:15, *"¹⁵Unto the pure all things are pure: but unto them that are defiled and unbelieving is nothing pure; but even their mind and **conscience** is defiled."*

2. Imagination:

1 Chronicles 28:9, *"⁹And thou, Solomon my son, know thou the God of thy father, and serve him with a perfect heart and with a willing mind: for the Lᴏʀᴅ searcheth all hearts, and understandeth all the **imaginations** of the thoughts:*

if thou seek him, he will be found of thee; but if thou forsake him, he will cast thee off forever."

2 Corinthians 10:4-5-"⁴*(For the weapons of our warfare are not carnal, but mighty through God to the pulling down of strong holds;)* ⁵*Casting down* **imaginations,** *and every high thing that exalteth itself against the knowledge of God, and bringing into captivity every thought to the obedience of Christ".*

3. Reason:

Isaiah 1:18-19, "¹⁸*Come now, and let us* **reason** *together, saith the* LORD*: though your sins be as scarlet, they shall be as white as snow; though they be red like crimson, they shall be as wool.*¹⁹*If ye be willing and obedient, ye shall eat the good of the land".*

Mark 2:8, "⁸*And immediately when Jesus perceived in his spirit that they so* **reasoned** *within themselves, he said unto them, Why reason ye these things in your hearts?"*

Acts 17:2, "*2And Paul, as his manner was, went in unto them, and three sabbath days **reasoned** with them out of the scriptures*".

4. Memory:

Proverbs 10:7, "*7The **memory** of the just is blessed: but the name of the wicked shall rot.*"

John 14:26, "*26But the Comforter, which is the Holy Ghost, whom the Father will send in my name, he shall teach you all things, and bring all things to your remembrance, whatsoever I have said unto you.*"

1 Corinthians 15:2, "*2By which also ye are saved, if ye keep in **memory** what I preached unto you, unless ye have believed in vain.*"

5. Affections:

Philippians 1:8, "*8For God is my witness, how greatly I long for you all with the **affection** of Jesus Christ.*"

Philippians 2:1, "*Therefore if there is any consolation in Christ, if any comfort of love, if* *any fellowship of the Spirit, if any **affection** and mercy".*

SPIRIT: **John 4:24,** "[24] God is a Spirit: and they that worship him must worship him in spirit and in truth."

THE SPIRIT HAS FIVE COMPONENTS

1. Faith:

Romans 10:17, "[17] *So then **faith** comes by hearing, and hearing by the word of God."*

Hebrews 11:1, *"Now **faith** is the substance of things hoped for, the evidence of things not seen."*

Hebrews 11:3, "[3] *By **faith** we understand that the [a]worlds were framed by the word of God, so that the things which are seen were not made of things which are visible."*

Hebrews 11:4,6, "*4By **faith** Abel offered to God a more excellent sacrifice than Cain, through which he obtained witness that he was righteous, God testifying of his gifts; and through it he being dead still speaks.*"

Hebrews 11:6, "*6But without **faith** it is impossible to please Him, for he who comes to God must believe that He is, and that He is a rewarder of those who diligently seek Him.*"

2. Hope:

Hebrews 6:19, "*19This **hope** we have as an anchor of the soul, both sure and steadfast, and which enters the Presence behind the veil*".

Psalm 130:5, "*5I wait for the LORD, my soul waits,*

*And in His word I do **hope**.*"

Psalm 71:5, "*For You are my **hope**, O Lord GOD;*

You are my trust from my youth."

Psalm 119:81, " *81* *My soul faints for Your salvation,*

But I **hope** *in Your word.*"

3. Prayer:

Luke 18:1, *"And he spake a parable unto them to this end, that men ought always to* **pray***, and not to faint".*

Matthew 6:9-13, *"9 In this manner, therefore,* **pray***:*

Our Father in heaven,
Hallowed be Your name.
10 Your kingdom come.
Your will be done
On earth as it is in heaven.
11 Give us this day our daily bread.
12 And forgive us our debts,
As we forgive our debtors.
13 And do not lead us into temptation,
But deliver us from the evil one.
For Yours is the kingdom and the power and the glory forever. Amen."

2 Chronicles 7:14, "*14 if My people who are called by My name will humble themselves, and **pray** and seek My face, and turn from their wicked ways, then I will hear from heaven, and will forgive their sin and heal their land.*"

Ephesians 6:18, "*18 **praying** always with all **prayer** and supplication in the Spirit, being watchful to this end with all perseverance and supplication for all the saints*".

Jeremiah 29:12, "*12 Then you will call upon Me and go and pray to Me, and I will listen to you.*"

4. **Reverence:** honor and respect that is deeply felt and outwardly demonstrated. Because of the Lord God's awesome power and majesty, He is deserving of the highest level of reverence

Leviticus 19:30, "*30 Ye shall keep my sabbaths, and **reverence** my sanctuary: I am the LORD.*"

Hebrews 12:28, "*28 Therefore, since we are receiving a kingdom which cannot be shaken,* let us have grace, by which we [a]*may serve God acceptably with* **reverence** *and godly fear."*

Ephesians 5:33, *"[33] Nevertheless let every one of you in particular so love his wife even as himself; and the wife see that she* **reverences** *her husband.,*

Psalm 89:7, *"[7] God is greatly to be feared in the assembly of the saints, and to be had in* **reverence** *of all them that are about him."*

5. Worship:

John 4:21-24, *"[21] Jesus saith unto her, Woman, believe me, the hour cometh, when ye shall neither in this mountain, nor yet at Jerusalem,* **worship** *the Father.*

[22] Ye **worship** *ye know not what: we know what we* **worship***: for salvation is of the Jews.*

[23] But the hour cometh, and now is, when the true **worshippers shall worship** *the Father in spirit and in truth: for the Father seeketh such* **to worship** *him.*

[24] *God is a Spirit: and they that* **worship** *him must* **worship** *him in spirit and in truth."*

Job 1:20, *"[20] Then Job arose, and rent his mantle, and shaved his head, and fell down upon the ground, and* **worshipped***".*

Psalm 95:6, *"[6] O come, let us* **worship** *and bow down: let us kneel before the* LORD *our maker."*

Deuteronomy 29:18, CSB, *"[18] Be sure there is no man, woman, clan, or tribe among you to-day whose heart turns away from the* LORD *our God to go and* **worship** *the gods of those nations. Be sure there is no root among you bearing poisonous and bitter fruit."*

Revelation 4:10-11, *"[10] The four and twenty elders fall down before him that sat on the throne, and* **worship** *him that liveth for ever and ever, and cast their crowns before the throne, saying,*

[11] Thou art worthy, O Lord, to receive glory and honour and power: for thou hast created all

things, and for thy pleasure they are and were created."

THE EXPERIENCES AFTER DEATH

What happens to the righteous soul during death? You will realize that you have died and are out of the body, and that you have reached paradise, and will know where you are to spend eternity.

What will be our first experiences be? **Our first experience** will be that death was so easy, it was like falling asleep and awakening in a beautiful world; that there was no "Valley of Death", and the ministering angels were waiting to carry us to paradise as they carried Lazarus.

Luke 16:22, *"22 And it came to pass, that the beggar died, and was carried by the angels into Abraham's bosom: the rich man also died, and was buried".*

Hebrew 1:13-14, "[13] *But to which of the angels said he at any time, sit on my right hand, until I make thine enemies thy footstool?*

[14] Are they not all ministering spirits, sent forth to minister for them who shall be heirs of salvation?"

What a delight it will be to meet our guardian angel who watched over us in our earth life.

Our second experience will be the consciousness of what we have left behind, our earthly body with all its weaknesses, sufferings, and limitations, and that we have a body that is absolutely well and fitted in every way for the spiritual realm in which it is to dwell.

2 Corinthians 5:1-2, "*For we know that if our earthly house of this tabernacle were dissolved, we have a building of God, a house not made with hands, eternal in the heavens.*

[2] For in this we groan, earnestly desiring to be clothed upon with our house which is from heaven".

1 Corinthians 15:47, "⁴⁷*The first man is of the earth, earthy; the second man is the Lord from heaven."*

Mark 14:58, "⁵⁸*We heard him say, I will destroy this temple that is made with hands, and within three days I will build another made without hands."*

Hebrews 9:24, "²⁴*For Christ is not entered into the holy places made with hands, which are the figures of the true; but into heaven itself, now to appear in the presence of God for us".*

Our Third Experience will be that we are being transported swiftly upward through the earth in real space toward a beautiful country whose radiance is brighter than the sun. And as we approach it, we will see, coming out to meet us and escort us home, groups of angels who sing, "Blessed are they that do his commandments, that they may have right to the tree of life and may enter in through the gates of the city."

Revelation 22:14, "¹⁴*Blessed are they that do his commandments, that they may have right to the tree of life, and may enter in through the gates into the city.*"

Hebrews 11:13-16, "¹³*These all died in faith, not having received the promises, but having seen them afar off, and were persuaded of them, and embraced them, and confessed that they were strangers and pilgrims on the earth.*

¹⁴*For they that say such things declare plainly that they seek a country.*

¹⁵*And truly, if they had been mindful of that country from whence, they came out, they might have had opportunity to have returned.*

¹⁶*But now they desire a better country, that is, a heavenly: wherefore God is not ashamed to be called their God: for he hath prepared for them a city.*"

Our Fourth Experience will be that we are in a new environment whose atmosphere is love, that there is no discord or lack of harmony in our new home, and that its chief characteristic is holiness.

1 John 4:15-16, "[15]*Whosoever shall confess that Jesus is the Son of God, God dwelleth in him, and he in God.*

[16]*And we have known and believed the love that God hath to us. God is love; and he that dwelleth in love dwelleth in God, and God in him."*

John 3:16, "[16]*For God so loved the world, that he gave his only begotten Son, that whosoever believeth in him should not perish, but have everlasting life."*

Our Fifth Experience will be the feeling that we are near to Jesus.

Luke 23:39-43, "[39]*And one of the malefactors which were hanged railed on him, saying, if thou be Christ, save thyself and us.*

[40]*But the other answering rebuked him, saying, Dost not thou fear God, seeing thou art in the same condemnation?*

⁴¹And we indeed justly; for we receive the due reward of our deeds: but this man hath done nothing amiss.

⁴²And he said unto Jesus, Lord, remember me when thou comest into thy kingdom.

⁴³And Jesus said unto him, Verily I say unto thee, today shalt thou be with me in paradise."

Revelation 2:7, *"⁷He that hath an ear, let him hear what the Spirit saith unto the churches; To him that overcometh will I give to eat of the tree of life, which is in the midst of the paradise of God."*

2 Corinthians 12:1-4, *"This is the third time I am coming to you. In the mouth of two or three witnesses shall every word be established.*

²I told you before, and foretell you, as if I were present, the second time; and being absent now I write to them which heretofore have sinned, and to all other, that, if I come again, I will not spare:

³Since ye seek a proof of Christ speaking in me, which to you-ward is not weak, but is mighty in you.

⁴For though he was crucified through weakness, yet he liveth by the power of God. For we also are weak in him, but we shall live with him by the power of God toward you."

1 Thessalonians 4:16-17, *"¹⁶For the Lord himself shall descend from heaven with a shout, with the voice of the archangel, and with the trump of God: and the dead in Christ shall rise first:*

¹⁷Then we which are alive and remain shall be caught up together with them in the clouds, to meet the Lord in the air: and so, shall we ever be with the Lord."

Our Sixth Experience will be that of meeting our loved ones.

Matthew 17:1-4, *"And after six days Jesus taketh Peter, James, and John his brother, and bringeth them up into a high mountain apart,*

²*And was transfigured before them: and his face did shine as the sun, and his raiment was white as the light.*

³*And, behold, there appeared unto them Moses and Elias talking with him.*

⁴*Then answered Peter, and said unto Jesus, Lord, it is good for us to be here: if thou wilt, let us make here three tabernacles; one for thee, and one for Moses, and one for Elias."*

Luke 24:36-39, "*³⁶And as they thus spake, Jesus himself stood in the midst of them, and saith unto them, Peace be unto you.*

³⁷*But they were terrified and affrighted, and supposed that they had seen a spirit.*

³⁸*And he said unto them, why are ye troubled? and why do thoughts arise in your hearts?*

³⁹*Behold my hands and my feet, that it is I myself: handle me, and see; for a spirit hath not flesh and bones, as ye see me have."*

John 20:19-20, "*19 Then the same day at evening, being the first day of the week, when the doors were shut where the disciples were assembled for fear of the Jews, came Jesus and stood in the midst, and saith unto them, Peace be unto you.*

20 And when he had so said, he shewed unto them his hands and his side. Then were the disciples glad, when they saw the LORD."

Romans 6:3-5, "*3 Know ye not, that so many of us as were baptized into Jesus Christ were baptized into his death?*

4 Therefore we are buried with him by baptism into death: that like as Christ was raised up from the dead by the glory of the Father, even so we also should walk in newness of life.

5 For if we have been planted together in the likeness of his death, we shall be also in the likeness of his resurrection".

Our Seventh Experience will be the meeting with the Saints who have preceded us to glory, such as the Patriarchs, Prophets, Apostles, and Christian leaders of our own day.

<u>JESUS CHRIST</u>

The first fruits of **1 Corinthians 15:22-23** with the Saints in **Matthew 27:50-53** are the first fruits Saints of old in **Ephesians 4:8-10**

1 Corinthians 15:22-23, "*[22] For as in Adam all die, even so in Christ shall all be made alive.*

[23] But every man in his own order: Christ the first fruits; afterward they that are Christ's at his coming."

Matthew 27:50-53, "*[50] Jesus, when he had cried again with a loud voice, yielded up the ghost.*

[51] And, behold, the veil of the temple was rent in twain from the top to the bottom; and the earth did quake, and the rocks rent;

⁵²And the graves were opened; and many bodies of the saints which slept arose,

⁵³And came out of the graves after his resurrection, and went into the holy city, and appeared unto many."

Ephesians 4:8-10, *"⁸Wherefore he saith, when he ascended up on high, he led captivity captive, and gave gifts unto men.*

⁹(Now that he ascended, what is it but that he also descended first into the lower parts of the earth?

¹⁰He that descended is the same also that ascended up far above all heavens, that he might fill all things.)"